The Cowboy's False Start

Cowboys of Whistle Rock Ranch
Book Two

Contemporary Western Romance

SHIRLEEN DAVIES

Book Series by Shirleen Davies

<u>Historical Western Romances</u>

Redemption Mountain
MacLarens of Fire Mountain Historical
MacLarens of Boundary Mountain

<u>Romantic Suspense</u>

Eternal Brethren Military Romantic Suspense
Peregrine Bay Romantic Suspense

<u>Contemporary Western Romance</u>

Cowboys of Whistle Rock Ranch
MacLarens of Fire Mountain Contemporary
Macklins of Whiskey Bend

The best way to stay in touch is to subscribe to my newsletter. Go to my Website **www.shirleendavies.com** and fill in your email and name in the
Join My Newsletter boxes. That's it!

Avalanche Ranch Press, LLC
PO Box 12618
Prescott, AZ 86304

Book design and conversions by Joseph Murray at 3rdplanetpublishing.com

Cover design by Sweet 'n Spicy Designs

ISBN: 978-1-947680-73-9

I care about quality, so if you find something in error, please contact me via email at shirleen@shirleendavies.com

Description

Two shattered hearts. A family with secrets. A second chance for this cowboy to fix the mistakes from his past and seize the future of his dreams.

Virgil Redstar has spent most of his life on Whistle Rock Ranch. Breeding and training some of the most spectacular Paint horses in the country tests his talent while soothing the hole in his soul. His return from college and promotion to foreman provides everything he needs. Almost.

Almost nine years after he shattered her heart, Lily Cardoza's life is a success. Her work as a nurse challenges and fulfills her. She enjoys rides with her best friend, Daisy Bonner, and occasional dates with eligible men. All is good in her world. Until the man she still loves presses for another chance.

Taking cautious steps, Virgil and Lily attempt to regain the relationship lost years ago. Rides on the ranch, dinners in town, and evenings spent together begin to heal the deep wounds which have never healed.

What neither Virgil nor Lily know are the dark secrets his father has never shared. Secrets which can end any plan for a second chance.

The Cowboy's False Start, book two in the Cowboys of Whistle Rock Ranch Contemporary Western Romance series, is a clean and wholesome, full-length novel with an HEA.

The Cowboy's
False Start

Chapter One

Whistle Rock Ranch
Early Spring...

Virgil gave his black and white Paint mare her head, leaning forward in the saddle, staying neck and neck with Wyatt as they raced toward the western border of the ranch. It had been too long since he'd taken time for himself, allowed himself to relax.

With a loud whoop, he urged his mare on, somewhat surprised when Wyatt's gelding, Mighty Quinn, fell back. They'd been best friends and frequent competitors since Virgil's father took a job as the ranch foreman when the boys were five. Lots had changed in twenty-three years, but not their friendship.

Spotting the boundary marker ahead, Virgil urged Migisi on. Exhilaration swept through him as he passed the rotting finish post they'd erected as teens. A second later, Wyatt joined him, both laughing.

If either Virgil's father, Jasper, or Wyatt's had seen their race, they'd be hearing about irresponsibility and immaturity for days. Those days were long gone.

Anson's serious heart attack months earlier, and Jasper's diagnosis of asthma, prompted Wyatt's promotion to ranch manager and Virgil's to foreman. Both were bittersweet changes.

"Good ride, Virg." Wyatt slid to the ground before clasping his friend's shoulder. "It's been too long."

Wyatt had returned from his honeymoon with Daisy days earlier, and still sported a broad smile. Wasting no time getting back to work, they'd scheduled themselves the chore of checking the western fence lines.

"Glad you and Daisy are back. It still feels strange to think of you as married."

Taking a swallow of water, he handed the bottle to Virgil. "It's no different for me. Didn't think I'd marry for years." Shrugging one shoulder, he slid the bottle into his saddlebag. "She's perfect for me, Virg."

"You don't have to convince me."

"Tell me what's been going on at the ranch."

"The wolf pack from last winter is back at it. They attacked a small herd of cattle. Left one dead and two injured. We got them back to the ranch and had the vet come out to patch them up. If there's no infection, they should be fine. Dorie's real good, Wyatt."

Dorothea Worrel had bought the veterinary clinic from the previous doctor over a year earlier, wasting no time embedding herself in the community. Even the few skeptical old-timers had been won over by her skills.

"Are you interested in her?" Wyatt stepped to the fence, checking the wire. "You could do a lot worse."

"She's a fine woman. Just not for me." Virgil retrieved tools from his saddlebags, handing one to Wyatt.

Taking the wire tightener, he locked gazes with Virgil. "Have you spoken with Lily?"

Without answering, he helped Wyatt with several more wires, straightening to look up at the bright blue sky. After a difficult winter, everyone hoped they'd be spared harsh, spring storms.

"I want to show you the location of the wolf attack."

Nodding, Wyatt let his question about Lily go. Virgil would talk when he was ready. Mounting, they followed the fence line north, making repairs where needed.

"It's up there." Virgil led him to a shallow gully. Red still stained the earth and rocks. "We buried the carcass, or what was left of it. Never saw the pack, but nothing else could've done the same damage. Dorie agreed the bites matched what she'd expect from a wolf. We may have a real problem, Wyatt. I reported it to Wyoming Game and Fish, let them know we'd file for compensation on the dead heifer."

"The attacks last winter were farther south. I'm not surprised they're moving north."

Leaning back in the saddle, Virgil looked around. "They'll migrate wherever is needed for food. There are plenty of deer and elk. I don't know why they're going after the cattle, other than opportunity. Our heifers are an easy target. I've been posting men around the herd." Shoving his hat down on his head, he gathered his reins. "You ready to head back?"

A smile crossed Wyatt's face. "Yep. I already miss my bride."

3

Laughing, Virgil reined Migisi toward the ranch.

Riding at a walk beside each other, Wyatt thought of his new role, and the added responsibilities. He'd already been tested when his parents went on their first cruise in January. All had gone well, in big part to Virgil's skills as the new foreman.

"Pop isn't settling into retirement as well as I'd hoped. I thought the vacation would give him time to adapt. Mom is frustrated trying to keep him out of my way."

"The ranch has been his life, as it has been for my father. Jasper is no more pleased about me taking over his foreman position as Anson is with you running ranch operations. Both were forced to back off because of health issues. My guess is we'll feel the same in thirty years."

"Thirty years..." Wyatt's voice trailed off. "Seems forever, yet I'm sure our fathers were surprised how fast the years passed. Jonah and Gage are driving in this weekend to go over the progress on our expanded operations. Gage is anxious to take reservations."

"We aren't ready. Maybe by mid-July, assuming we have enough reservations." Virgil's duties would be to continue the breeding and training programs, while offering trail rides and lessons to their guests. He welcomed the expansion of duties, the challenge of making all the pieces work together.

"Have you had any luck locating someone to work alongside you?"

Mouth twisting into a grimace, Virgil let his grip on the reins loosen. "I don't know why Barrel can't be our man. He's been at the ranch almost as long as you and me."

"Barrel's a great guy. Dependable, good with the men, and an excellent trainer."

"But?"

"He's a little deficient in the charm category. We need someone who the guests gravitate toward."

"Barrel is a real likeable cowboy."

"Never said he wasn't." Ducking his head, Wyatt considered how he could describe his reasons for wanting someone different than Barrel. "We need someone men trust and women find fascinating."

Throwing back his head, Virgil roared in laughter. "Fascinating?"

"Sure. Charming, captivating. Whatever you want to call it. A man who knows his boundaries."

"A married man," Virgil offered.

"Might be best. I'll leave that up to you. What's the latest on you and Lily?" Wyatt felt bad about how little time he'd spent with his friend before the wedding. Especially about Virgil's relationship with the woman he'd dated for two years in high school. He'd graduated a year before her, deciding it best to break up before leaving for college. Virgil regretted the decision right away. Eight years later, she still had a difficult time being around him.

Virgil wondered how long Wyatt would wait to ask again about the woman driving him crazy. "There is no me and Lily. She's dating, and refuses to speak with me."

"Dating who?"

"A doctor at the hospital. The assistant director of the Chamber of Commerce. And I think she's seeing a rancher from south of town."

Wyatt couldn't stifle a surprised chuckle. "Three different men?"

"That's what I've heard. For a woman who dated almost no one for eight years, she's making up for it now." Virgil's voice held no humor. "I should've done something as soon as she returned from nursing school. But Lily was so angry, refused to be anywhere near me. Guess nothing's changed."

"You made progress with her last Thanksgiving while she and Daisy recuperated at the ranch after their accident. You hardly left Lily's bedside."

"I'm pretty sure the time I spent with Emma didn't go over well." Virgil mentioned Emma Griffin, the young woman hired to help their main cook, Nacho. "It meant nothing. She's a single mother on her own for the first time. I'd keep her company in the kitchen while Lily slept. Nacho was almost always with us." Glancing away, he massaged the back of his neck. "She gave me a great book on holistic animal medicine. I gave Emma and Koa presents for Christmas, but not Lily. How could I have forgotten her?"

Reining to a stop, he removed his hat, running a hand through silky, black hair, which plunged to halfway down his back. Reaching into a pocket for a leather thong, he gathered his hair, securing it with the thin strap.

"I don't know how I could've messed up so badly. Guess it was a false start." Clucking, Migisi continued toward the barn.

"You need to be honest with her, Virgil. Lily needs to know you still love her. That you've always loved her. My confession worked with Daisy. No reason it won't work with her best friend."

Settling his hat back on his head, Virgil considered Wyatt's words. "You hadn't been seeing Daisy long before leaving for Montana State University. I understand she fell in love with you back then, and never met another man who held her interest. Lily and I were together two years before I left. We loved each other, talked about marriage and children after we both graduated from college. I'll never forget the look on her face when I broke up with her."

"You blindsided Lily."

"I was young and stupid, but I did love her. Still do. I doubt she'll ever trust me again."

They rode in silence for several minutes before Wyatt spoke again.

"Maybe it's time for you to date."

Shaking his head, Virgil chuckled at what he considered a ridiculous idea. "I'm working fourteen-hour days, which will increase once we get the loan for the new operations. I expect sixteen to eighteen hours will become a normal day during the spring and summer. There won't be time for dating, or much else. Which is fine with me. I don't have the interest to get involved with anyone."

"What if Lily changes her mind?"

"She won't."

"But what if she decides to start talking to you?"

"I'll talk to her. Doesn't mean anything will come of it."

"You're being stubborn, my friend."

"I'm being realistic. It's been eight years, Wyatt. She's moving on, and as soon as the interest hits me, I will too. Don't forget Brilliance doesn't have a broad selection of eligible women."

Rubbing his jaw, Wyatt grinned. "Well now, there's Dorie. A beautiful woman with her own business."

"Not gonna happen. There's no spark."

"What about the woman who opened the flower shop in town. Tall, slender, great laugh." Wyatt's mouth twisted into a grimace. "Wish I could think of her name."

"I've met her. Same as Dorie. No spark."

"I heard there's a new school teacher at the elementary school."

"She's engaged."

"How about Emma?"

"Nope. She's a wonderful woman who'll be right for someone. Just not me. When I'm ready to date again, I'll pick the woman."

The sound of an engine drew their attention toward a lone figure on a small dirt bike. A plume of dust rose from the rear tire as it came straight toward them. Disappearing down a gully, the young rider lifted his hand to wave when the bike hit a bump, throwing him over the handlebars.

Moving their mounts into a gallop, the two men covered the distance between themselves and Emma's eight-year-old boy in record time.

"You all right, Koa?" Wyatt asked as he slid to the ground.

"Great. Did you see me?" He raised both arms in the air. "I'm going to be a pro one day."

Picking up the bike, Virgil recalled a time years ago when he and Wyatt said the same. Maybe this young boy, covered in dirt with a broad smile and an open future, would find a way to make his dream happen.

Chapter Two

Pushing the food around on a plate much too big for the small portions, Lily listened to her date. He'd been explaining a new program at the Chamber of Commerce for at least twenty minutes, threatening to put her to sleep.

She'd already nodded off once, awaking within seconds. So caught up in his own story, he hadn't noticed her eyes close.

"What do you think, Lillian?"

Startled, she set her fork down for what would be the last time. She'd asked him more than once to call her Lily. He'd responded by telling her Lillian suited her better. An elegant name for an elegant woman.

"Think about what?"

"The new program. Specifically..."

Her mind wandered again as he began another long explanation of what he'd already described. Lifting her glass of water, Lily's gaze wandered to the front door. Two men walked in, followed by Wyatt and Daisy. She knew all of them. Wyatt's brothers, Jonah and Gage, spoke as the hostess sat them at a table for five. That's when she saw the last member of their party, Virgil Redstar, enter. She steeled herself against the wave of painful feelings. Years had passed since he'd stopped seeing her, yet the crack in her heart had never healed.

The group's appearance brought a smile to her face, relieving the boredom of a date Lily wished she hadn't accepted. They were seated across the room, none of them noticing her.

Wyatt and Daisy had returned from their honeymoon two weeks earlier. So far, she and Daisy had spoken on the phone, their schedules not allowing them to see each other. She missed her best friend.

Their time together had become sparse ever since his marriage proposal. Daisy's mother-in-law, Margie Bonner, had taken charge of the planning. Instead of helping her best friend with the arrangements, Lily had been left out of everything except the dress fitting and a few insignificant activities. The entire experience had stung, although she'd never voiced her disappointment to Daisy.

"Did you hear me, Lillian?"

Moving her attention to her date, she shook her head. "I'm sorry. Guess all those extra shifts at the hospital are catching up with me. It may be best for me to head home instead of being such a lousy date."

"If you're sure."

"I am."

"I'll drive you home."

Relief spread through her, all except the driving home part. "No need. I walked here from my apartment. It's very close." She'd moved out of her tiny place near the hospital a month before Daisy's wedding, choosing a two bedroom, two bath apartment in downtown.

"I'll walk you home and come back for my car." Standing, he walked around the table, helping with her lightweight coat.

Not wanting to draw attention to them, she accepted his offer. "Let's leave through their side door. It's closer to my place."

He tried twice to slip his hand into hers on the short walk to her apartment. The first time, she'd pulled her hand away. A phone call had saved her the second time. Seeing Daisy's face on the screen, she smiled while not answering.

"Here we are. Thanks so much for dinner." Taking a few steps away to avoid an awkward goodnight kiss, she wrapped her hand around the gate to her front door. "I had a good time."

"I'd like to see you again, Lily. May I call you?"

"Of course." A call would give her time to come up with a kind way to let him down. Opening the gate, she slipped into the small front patio. "Thank you again for dinner and walking me home."

Hearing his faint goodnight, she felt a pang of guilt. He was a nice man, just not for her. Making her way into the large kitchen, she slipped out of her coat before making a cup of tea.

Her thoughts moved to Virgil. He'd been handsome in high school. Over eight years later, he transitioned to being one of the most gorgeous, single men in Brilliance. She knew it for a fact.

The women at work talked about him with awe in their voices. The first time she'd heard them discuss eligible men, he'd been mentioned, along with Wyatt and a few others. It had been the same in college.

A year younger than him, Lily had attended the University of Wyoming, the same as Daisy, Jonah, Gage, and Virgil. It had been hard enough seeing him around campus, seeing him hang out with other women.

During those years, he'd asked her to join him for concerts, hiking trips, and horseback rides. She'd always refused. No matter how hard she tried, Lily could never make the transition to being just a friend.

Taking her tea into the living room, she grabbed the controller, selecting a sitcom about life in a small town. She'd watched a few episodes, and like tonight, it hadn't held her attention.

Hitting the power button, her gaze moved to the bookcase she'd purchased a week earlier. She'd filled it with books, framed pictures, and items collected while in school. One object in particular caught her attention.

Setting the tea aside, Lily picked up the hand crafted wooden horse, studying it as she had so many times over the last eight years. Virgil had given it to her for her birthday, a few weeks before he'd told her they had to break up.

Holding the carving, she ran her thumb over the smooth wood. Those had been wonderful times—high school, their entire lives ahead of them. She and Virgil had been together two years. A year younger than him, Lily had believed everything he said. When he'd spoken of getting married after he graduated from college, she'd held his words close to her heart. At seventeen, she knew he'd never lie to her.

"How young and stupid you were," Lily muttered to herself.

Taking a last look at the carving, she returned it to the bookshelf, shoving it to the back. Hesitating for a moment, she picked up a picture of her and Daisy, placing it to block her view of the carving.

Turning around, she looked around the apartment. It had taken six months before there'd been a vacancy. She'd loved it the moment the owner opened the front door. A month had passed since that day. One month of extra shifts at the hospital, dates with men who didn't hold her interest, and long nights sitting alone in an apartment too big for one person.

Daisy's marriage had changed Lily's life so much more than expected. Since announcing their engagement, the two women had spent less than a half dozen days together.

In less than a heartbeat, the attention Virgil showered on her after the accident last Thanksgiving had moved to Emma. Lily wondered if they'd been dating.

She had other friends, though most were married, some with children. None knew her as well as Daisy. Lily had to accept their days of meeting for dinner, wine and cheese at one of their homes, or sleepovers with ice cream and a movie, were long gone.

Spotting her laptop on the kitchen table, an idea began to form. Other than Daisy, she had no ties in Brilliance. She didn't own a house or have a boyfriend. The job she loved could be duplicated in any of a dozen towns in Wyoming.

Entering search terms, her eyes widened at the results. There were dozens of postings for nurses throughout the state. Some in doctor's offices, a good number in hospitals, and a few for individual patients.

Printing the list, she circled those of interest. Making another cup of tea, she studied the openings, trying to picture herself in the various towns. She preferred to stay in western Wyoming, close enough for a short drive to Brilliance. Lily also wanted a larger town where there were more eligible men.

After eight years, it was time to forge her own future while burying memories of what she'd shared with Virgil.

Stirring a bit of sugar and touch of cream into his coffee, Virgil listened to Jonah explaining the latest cashflow projections for their new venture. Gage had already provided his updated information for the western adventure, offering individual selections guests could make to enhance their vacation.

Wyatt and Virgil provided updates on the horses they'd selected for trail rides and lessons. They hadn't hired a head wrangler to lead the rides. For now, Virgil would add that position to his long list of responsibilities.

He could feel the undercurrent of excitement around the table. They all believed the expansion would be successful, entice visitors who sought a little more than the standard dude ranch experience.

Glancing at the side door, the image of Lily sneaking out with her date brought a slight smile. He'd spotted her through the front window when arriving with the others.

Wyatt's words came back to him.

"You need to be honest with her, Virgil. Lily needs to know you still love her. That you've always loved her."

Good advice if you were talking about a woman willing to listen. Lily couldn't stand being in the same restaurant with him. Forget catching her alone to explain how he felt, and set her straight on his relationship with Emma.

They were friends. Nothing more. Not that Lily would ever believe him.

Chapter Three

"It's the spring cattle drive, Lily. Everyone will be involved. You have to come out and ride with us."

Lowering herself onto a chair in the hospital cafeteria, Lily sipped a cup of coffee. It had been a long shift, with three hours to go. The next three days were her own, and she had a long to-do list. Number one was updating her resume.

"I don't know, Daisy. I've been taking extra shifts to save money. I'm exhausted."

"It's one long day. The second day, we vaccinate the cattle, so you don't have to stay for that. We're moving the cattle from the north pasture to one farther south. We leave at sunrise and return close to sunset. There'll be a barbecue afterward. I'd really like you to come."

"I'm not sure." Lips pressed into a tight line, she wasn't quite ready to address the real issue.

"He isn't interested in Emma."

"How do you know?"

"Because Virgil asks about you all the time. I know the last few months haven't been what you expected."

"Daisy, he hasn't spoken more than a few dozen words to me since Christmas. He's had more than enough chances. When I'm around, he spends all his time with

Emma and Koa, or with the ranch hands. It's as if I'm invisible. Maybe I am. I've got to get back upstairs."

"At least think about coming out. It's in two days."

"All right. I'll think about it, but no promises. If I come, it won't be to see Virgil. It'll be to spend time with you."

"I can live with that."

"I'll call you tomorrow." Ending the call, Lily slid the phone in a pocket as she thought about joining her best friend on the cattle drive.

She'd been on them before, some three days long as they moved herds between pastures. Those often included several ranches, everyone working together to finish the work in a shorter period of time.

Lily loved being involved in the drives, helping vaccinate the cattle, doing whatever was needed during her time on the range. While in high school, she'd ridden alongside Virgil. He'd encouraged her, shared much of what he knew about horses and cattle.

For a time, she'd considered veterinary medicine, the same as Virgil. After he'd broke up with her, she'd tossed aside the idea and pursued nursing.

She couldn't ask for a better job or more competent doctors. It surprised her how accomplished, big city docs left to take jobs in small towns, such as Brilliance. Most stayed, especially those who weren't already married. If they left, it often was due to their spouses being unhappy with the change.

Before reaching the elevator to her department, noise from the emergency room drew her attention. Loud voices turned to shouts and cursing. Concerned, she rushed down the hall, opening the door to see the area in chaos.

Wide-eyed nurses stood to the side, listening to the four burly cowboys with bloodstained clothing. Those were the angry voices she'd heard. Two stood, while the other two had been placed on beds.

The one doctor on duty ordered the nurses to help. Instead of stepping forward, they moved farther away. Embarrassed at the inaction of her coworkers, Lily hurried to the first bed.

"What can I do, doctor?" She shot a disgusted look at the other nurses, who forgot their initial concern and moved to the second bed.

"Nothing," the patient yelled. "My horses. They need help more than me."

Her brows scrunched together. "Horses?"

"These men were in an accident. From what I understand, they were pulling a loaded horse trailer. The EMTs and sheriff's deputies arrived before the men could help their stock."

"Just patch me up and let me get back to the accident."

The man on the second bed grunted, letting them know he felt the same. Lily moved to his bedside, cleaning open wounds in preparation for the sutures she knew were needed.

The doctor shook his head. "You've got a concussion, cracked ribs, broken arm, and possible internal injuries. Your friend on the other bed is in a little better shape, but not much. I've ordered x-rays and tests for all four of you."

One of the men who stood nearby stepped forward. "I don't need no tests. Banged my head and twisted an ankle, but that's not enough to keep me here."

"Same here," the last of the four said, rubbing a shoulder.

Lily's gaze moved over him, thinking he might be right. Still, tests were needed to determine if there was internal damage.

"Have you placed sutures or used staples, Nurse Cardoza?"

"Yes, under a doctor's supervision."

"Are you comfortable closing your patient's wounds?" He spoke as he used staples to close his patient's lacerations.

A slight grin tipped up the corners of her mouth. "Yes, sir."

"Good. Get started and I'll check your work when I'm finished here."

She worked with careful diligence, finalizing the last injury as the doctor walked around the beds to stand next to her. Studying the placement of the staples, he nodded.

"Excellent. You've done this a few times. Am I right?"

"As a nurse, twice. At my friend's ranch, three times. Those weren't with staples."

A chuckle burst past his lips. "Animals or humans?"

Smiling, she looked up at him. "Humans. Can that be our secret?"

Returning her smile, he nodded. "Your secrets are safe with me."

Two aides pushed gurneys through the double doors. The taller spoke to the doctor. "These the two patients who need tests?"

"Yes. Plus, I want MRIs on those two."

"I said I don't need tests. I've got to get back to the accident."

Before the doctor could object, the two men shoved their way past the gurneys, exiting into the hospital hallway. Letting out a sigh, he pursed his lips, locking his weary gaze on the aides.

"All right. These two are ready to go with you."

Lily waited until the patients were wheeled out of the room before turning toward the doctor. "I do understand their reasons for leaving."

"So do I." Stretching the aching muscles in his neck, his hard gaze locked on the other nurses. "I understand your fear at what happened. However, it's your job to get over it and help the patients. If you can't, then emergency may not be the best department for you."

Lily's stomach clenched at the varied expressions on the nurses' faces. One, a woman she'd known since starting at the hospital, appeared crestfallen, while the other woman's expression steeled in anger.

"You can't speak to me as if I don't know what I'm doing."

"I can't speak to your competency since you didn't do your job with those patients."

The woman crossed her arms, one hip hitching out. "I'll be speaking with my supervisor about your accusations."

"So will I." He shifted to look at Lily. "Thank you for responding, Nurse Cardoza."

"Glad I was leaving the cafeteria when the shouts came. I'd better get back to my floor."

"Let me know if you need me to speak with your supervisor."

"Thank you, doctor. It shouldn't be an issue."

Through the remainder of her shift, Lily couldn't stop thinking about what happened in emergency. She enjoyed the challenge and quick action required dealing with trauma.

Her prior experience had included little time in a crisis environment. Today's situation reminded her how much she enjoyed working in fast-paced situations.

Before heading home, she poked her head into her supervisor's office to ask about the prospect of transferring. Even if she took a job in another city, whatever experience she gained from working in a trauma environment would be beneficial.

Leaving the supervisor's office, she walked straight to human resources. Filling out the required paperwork, she waited while the HR manager checked her record. Making two calls, she ended the last one with a smile. Lily would report to the emergency department when she returned from her three days off.

Driving home, Lily felt lighter than she had in a long time. A small step had been taken to change her life. Most people wouldn't see it as making a big difference. After several years of living in the past, wishing for something that would never come, she'd taken a positive step toward a better future.

Waking at four o'clock on the morning of the cattle drive, Lily dressed in jeans, a long-sleeved shirt, sweater, and boots. Eating a quick breakfast, she slipped into the jacket worn when working at the ranch. Grabbing her hat and prepacked backpack, she drove toward the Bonners'.

The sun hadn't shown its face when she parked beside a line of trucks. Lights outside and inside the barn illuminated the entire area, making an easy trek to where several groups stood together drinking coffee.

"Lily! You made it." Daisy ran toward her, arms extended to pull her friend into a hug. "I'm so glad you're here. I made it clear the two of us are to be in the same group." She glanced at the backpack. "You brought snacks?"

"A few power bars, water, brownies, and blondies. And yes, there's enough for both of us. Hopefully, there are saddlebags."

Slipping her arm through Lily's, Daisy led her toward the row of already saddled horses. "You're riding Jiminy, a six-year-old Paint gelding. He's gorgeous. I think we should work out a plan for you to buy him."

Laughing, Lily spotted the horse next to Daisy's mare, Honey. "Let's see how today goes." She wouldn't tell her friend about the resumes ready to upload for jobs as far away as Laramie and Sheridan.

"He sure is handsome." Lily ran her hand along Jiminy's neck several times. "Under fifteen hands?"

"Yep. Virgil will know for sure."

Lily planned to stay far away from him during the next fourteen hours. "That's all right. Was Jiminy your idea?"

Daisy stared past her, not meeting her gaze. "Not really."

"Probably Barrel. He knows the kind of horse I prefer riding." Something in Daisy's expression told her it wasn't the longtime ranch hand.

"I'll need to check with Wyatt. He's going to make some announcements before we ride out."

"I'll wait for you here, Daisy."

Ignoring those around her, Lily filled the saddlebags before tying a bandana around her neck. She'd learned the hard way how important they were when moving cattle.

"Jiminy should be perfect for you."

Stilling at the familiar voice, she sucked in a breath. Continuing to fill the saddlebags, she folded her backpack, stuffing it around the bottles of water.

"Fourteen-three."

She glanced over her shoulder at Virgil. "What?"

"He's fourteen-three hands. I've been training him since I returned to the ranch after college."

Forcing herself to relax, she again ran her hand down Jiminy's neck. "He's gorgeous. I'm surprised no one's bought him."

"This guy isn't for sale."

Brow lifting, she kept her focus on the gelding. "I thought all the horses were trained to sell."

"Not this one. I trained him for a particular person." Placing his hand over hers, he guided her to the horse's cheek.

He was so close, his warm breath washed across her face and neck. Her heart slammed against her chest. "Who did you train him for?"

Virgil waited, one...two...three beats. "Jiminy's for you, Lily."

Chapter Four

Heart hammering, Lily's throat constricted, making it hard to breathe. She needed space. Pulling her hand free, she stepped away, not yet meeting his searching gaze. She knew what the ranch charged for horses trained by Virgil. Some of their cutting horses went for tens of thousands of dollars.

"I don't have the money for one of your horses."

"Jiminy is a gift."

"What? No. I couldn't accept him as a gift. A quality horse, trained by you, is worth, well...too much to accept as a gift."

Running his hand along the gelding's flank, he murmured something to Jiminy, who reared his head and whinnied. "He's perfect for you. It was clear to me the first time I saw him prance around the corral. Let me do this for you, Lily."

The last words brought back the reason they could never have a future. "Why? Because you still feel guilty for dumping me in high school? Or is it because you're seeing Emma? Or is there another reason?" She held up a hand. "Don't answer. We were done a long time ago. You can see whoever you want." Turning, she got a couple feet away before he caught her arm.

"Stop, Lily. I want to answer your questions."

"This isn't a great time."

Letting go of her arm, he didn't step away. "We won't leave for another half hour. I know, since Wyatt and I created the schedule."

"Fine. Answer the questions, then leave me alone."

This wasn't how Virgil wanted this conversation to go, with Lily angry, her mind already closed to what he'd say. "You might be right. We can talk about this tonight."

"You know, all I want to understand is why. That's it. I don't care about you and Emma, or any woman you've seen since high school. Just tell me why you broke up with me. You owe me that much."

Besides being a conversation he wasn't anxious to have, the why of their breakup would take more than a few minutes. "That will take more than a few minutes."

Looking away, she gave a slow shake of her head. "I should've known."

"Known what?"

"That I'll never learn the truth. Which is lived without it a long time, Virgil."

"There you are." Barrel rushed toward them ready to go over the schedule. He'd like you there

"I should finish packing the saddlebags." H Lily offered a small smile to Barrel before leav alone.

Watching her leave, Virgil felt the punch of It had been months since he'd been so close to h a whiff of apples and honey, which set her a other women. He'd become accustomed to m

27

since he'd done as his father insisted. Virgil had also hated himself more every day for not refusing the order.

Lily wished she'd never agreed to participate on the cattle drive. Her heart still ached at the encounter with Virgil. She never should've mentioned Emma or anything else. Staying guarded, keeping questions to herself, had saved her a great deal of additional pain over the years since he'd left for college.

His appearance by her side today, the offer of Jiminy, pierced the shield meant to protect her heart. Would she never get over losing Virgil?

Riding next to Daisy, Lily forced away thoughts of the man she'd loved most of her life. "How long before we reach the herd?"

"Wyatt said less than two hours. Which will give us time to catch up. First, tell me what went on with you and Virgil before we left." Daisy flashed her a mischievous grin, the one signaling she wanted to know everything.

"Did you know he trained Jiminy with the intent of giving him to me?" Patting the gelding's neck, she thought of Virgil's hand on hers, the warmth which spread through her.

"I knew he trained him. He said Jiminy would be the perfect horse for you. I had no idea his intent was to offer him as a gift. Tell me you said yes."

"We didn't have what you'd describe as a regular conversation."

"You never do."

"I told him no. It's no secret a horse trained by Virgil goes for thousands of dollars. I can't accept such a valuable horse."

Pressing her lips together, Daisy nodded. "I'm not surprised. Still, you have to know there's a reason he took years training him for you."

"Guilt."

"For what?"

"Breaking up with me. Making me believe he still had feelings for me after our accident. For having an interest in Emma. Maybe not seeking me out in the last six months. Why else would he offer such an incredible horse to me?"

"Because he still loves you?"

Lily's chuckle held little humor. "He has a strange way of showing it. Whatever the reason, I can't accept the horse."

"Yes, you can. And you should. Jiminy is an amazing animal. I've seen Virgil work him. Besides being gorgeous, he's trained as a cutter, barrel racer, and working ranch horse. Accept him, Lily. Who knows? It may lead to you and Virgil sorting things out. I mean, if that's what you want."

Did she? Lily honestly had no answer.

The sound of approaching horses had the women glancing over their shoulders. "What are they doing here?" Lily muttered before she could stop herself.

Virgil and Wyatt closed the distance within a minute, taking positions on either side of the women. Much the same as bookends.

Not surprising, Virgil had chosen to ride next to Lily. "How's Jiminy doing?"

"Hard to tell, as we've only walked. Once we reach the cattle, I'll know more."

"No better time than now to try him out. Do you trust me enough to follow?"

She might not trust him with her heart, but he'd never do anything to put her in danger.

"Lily?"

"Yes. I trust you enough to follow your trail."

He studied her a moment, as if judging her sincerity. "We won't take a direct route, as I want Jiminy to cover more difficult terrain. Wyatt, Lily and I are going to ride ahead. We'll meet you at the herd. Let's go, Ms. Cardoza."

Clucking, Migisi moved into a jog, Jiminy and Lily right behind them. Catching up to ride next to him, she shot a quick glance at Virgil, noting the broad grin on his face.

He'd once told her it was impossible to be upset when on a horse. At the thought of that conversation, a smile crossed her own face. Virgil was right. Riding swept away whatever weighed on a person's mind.

It did for Lily as she rode alongside the man who'd broken her heart so many years earlier. For now, she'd forget their bittersweet history and free herself from the pain of their shared past.

Jiminy turned out to be a wonderful mount, with a smooth gait and calm disposition. When Virgil moved Migisi into a lope, she did the same with her gelding, Jiminy moving seamlessly into the faster gait.

Air rushed from her lungs as exhilaration claimed her. Noting Virgil veer to the left, she reined her horse to follow, continuing as he led Migisi into a path skirting the forest. Slowing to a jog, then a walk, she relaxed, feeling a sense of peace at the beauty around her.

Wildflowers of blue, white, yellow, and pink created an almost dizzying rush of color. It had been too long since she'd ventured out in the spring to enjoy the transition from the snows of winter.

"Beautiful, isn't it?"

Glancing up, she saw Virgil turning in his saddle to watch her. "Yes. I'd forgotten about all the wildflowers on the ranch."

Features sobering, Virgil gave a slow nod before shifting forward. It was his fault Lily didn't feel comfortable coming out to the ranch. She didn't want to run into him. She could barely talk to him after all this time.

He knew some on the ranch thought her animosity toward him should've died after so long. Virgil knew better, understood the deep hurt he'd caused. They'd been much more than two teenagers in love. He and Lily were soulmates, put on the earth to build a life together.

Pledging themselves to each other during the summer between his junior and senior year in high school, they knew nothing would ever come between them. With his father acting as chaperone, he'd taken Lily to the Northern Cheyenne Fourth of July Powwow a week later, explaining the events and ceremonies.

The summer and following year had been magical as their love grew. How could Virgil have known his father would forbid their union? Years later, Jasper had still never disclosed the reason.

Reining Migisi to a stop, he swept his left leg over the mare's neck, sliding to the ground. "Come on. I want to show you something."

She didn't ask any questions, simply followed him along a narrow path which led through groupings of immense boulders. Lily hadn't realized such terrain existed at Whistle Rock Ranch.

"We're almost there." On instinct, he slowed his pace, reaching out to take Lily's hand.

Dragging him to a stop, she peered down at their entwined fingers, knowing she should pull away. The familiar warmth of his hand, the jolt of power so strong she couldn't name it, flared up her arm. It had always been this way. Even if it meant little to Virgil, Lily found she had no desire to break the contact.

Taking a path around the boulders, he came to an abrupt stop. "You should be able to see it from here." He tugged her to his side.

"Oh, my gosh." The air whooshed from her lungs at the sight before her. What she thought was a simple grouping of boulders on their side changed to a sheer bluff overlooking the river below. The drop-off had to be at least fifty feet. "I had no idea this was here."

"Most people don't. Wyatt and I found it on one of his few visits home from his uncle's. Can you see just around the corner?" Moving her in front of him, he rested one hand on her shoulder while pointing with the other. "It's at the tip of my finger."

Eyes locked on the direction where he pointed, her jaw dropped on a gasp. "It's a nest."

"A special nest, Lily."

She glanced at him before looking back at the nest. "Special because?"

"It's for the eggs of a golden eagle." Reaching into a back pocket, he pulled out a pair of compact binoculars. "Use these."

Holding them to her eyes, she adjusted them before looking back at him with wide eyes. "There are eggs."

"They weren't there two weeks ago."

Taking one more look, she handed the binoculars back to Virgil. "When will they hatch?"

"Forty to forty-five days. I plan to ride back in a few weeks."

Bouncing on the balls of her boots, she couldn't contain an excited smile. "I'm coming with you."

Lowering the binoculars, his mouth slipped into a tight line before a tentative grin appeared. "I'd like that."

His gaze locked onto hers, neither looking away as seconds ticked by. Swallowing the ball of stark desire, he began to lower his head. He waited for her to look away, put distance between them. To his surprise, she stared, as if daring him to kiss her.

Before he could change his mind, Virgil's lips brushed over hers, the touch light, caressing. He wanted more, not daring to push her too fast. When she continued to watch him, he covered her mouth with his.

Chapter Five

The kiss was the same as Lily remembered. Warm, intense, causing heat to flash from her face to the tips of her purple painted toes. Gripping his muscled arms, she leaned into Virgil, a sigh escaping when he deepened the kiss.

Memories of their time together flooded back. Long rides on the ranch, walks around town, trips to rodeos, and kissing. Lots of kissing and holding hands. Then he'd ended everything.

The last pierced the haze of his closeness, reminding her of the pain his decision caused. Slowly pushing away, she let go of his arms while inhaling a slow breath.

Virgil said nothing, watching the play of emotions flicker across her face. He knew, without asking, Lily's mind had gone to their past. She turned toward their horses.

"We should leave to meet with the others."

Grateful she hadn't protested their kiss was a mistake, he followed, his heart slamming inside his chest. Virgil hadn't expected her to lean into him, return the passion as if they'd never been apart.

Watching her mount Jiminy, his breath caught on the fluid motion. She'd never been on a horse before meeting

Virgil. He'd been the first to introduce her to ranch life, the first to teach her to ride, the first to date her, the first to kiss her.

"Do you want to take the lead, Virgil?" She looked over her shoulder at him, nothing in her expression indicating she'd been affected by their kiss. Virgil knew otherwise. Her eyes always gave Lily away.

Clucking, he moved beside her. "I'll guide us back to the main trail, then you take over. I want to watch how you handle Jiminy."

"I'm not accepting him as a gift."

"I thought you'd say that." But there was a smile in his voice, as if he knew something she didn't.

"Really, Virgil. I know you can get thousands for him."

"You're worth thousands, Lily." His voice held a wistful tone.

Wide eyes shot to his, disbelief clear in the set of her mouth. Instead of answering, she stared at the reins in her hands, doing her best to hide the burn of tears at the back of her eyes.

"I know it will take a long time to make up for the hurt I've caused. I also know you may never trust me again. You should understand I won't give up trying to win you back. I'll never give up on us."

The words were soft, intimate, and tore at her heart. She'd waited a long time to hear him admit his intentions. The prospect of getting back together floated in the air, a promise or a warning? Lily wasn't sure. Did she have the courage to explore the difference?

Glancing up, relief soared through her. The trail leading to the herd couldn't be more than fifty yards ahead. Feeling his hot gaze on her face, she urged Jiminy into a jog, knowing Virgil could sense her discomfort.

Grateful at the distance he allowed between them, her breaths evened out as the knot in her stomach eased. He couldn't mean what he said. Not after all this time. Not after the attention he'd paid Emma.

The cook's assistant, short and petite, with large brown eyes and an oval face, would turn most heads. Lily heard more than one ranch hand had asked her to dinner. She could understand Virgil's interest in the woman. Even with a young son, her quiet, unassuming manner would appeal to him.

She'd seen Virgil and Koa together. It hadn't taken long for the impressionable eight year old to develop an intense case of hero worship. Daisy had mentioned how Koa followed him around, as would a puppy, intent on every word Virgil uttered. Everything about Emma and Koa spoke of family.

Family had become important to Virgil. His mother had walked out on him and his father on his fifth birthday. She'd given the excuse of picking up the cake before driving away in their fifteen-year-old Chrysler. Monica Redstar had never returned.

His life at Whistle Rock Ranch had provided the family he believed had been torn from him. Margie had taken the place of his missing mother, while Wyatt, Jonah, and Gage had become his brothers. It also left him with a strong desire to have his own family one day. Emma and Koa would appeal to the hole in his life left by a woman who'd abandoned him.

Lily's stomach plummeted. She had little to offer him. Her parents had died years earlier in a horrible two-car accident on their way to her college graduation.

She'd been left their old, much neglected house, a tiny savings account, and two small life insurance policies. Without enough funds to patch up the home she'd grown up in, Lily had sold it, adding the funds to her moderate savings.

Long hours at the hospital, an apartment downtown, and sad social life couldn't compete with the winsome Emma. Daisy believed the woman would take over for Nacho, who'd been toying with retirement for a while.

If Emma stayed, she'd become a fixture at the ranch, would rule the kitchen, and become the queen of meals. The perfect fit for a cowboy who loved the ranch and craved a family.

Her mind turned to their kiss, face heating at the memory. Setting out that morning, Lily never dreamed she'd be riding with Virgil, or that their day would include a brain-numbing kiss. It felt incredible. All she remembered, and every sensation she'd missed when he'd walked away.

Her jaw clenched as her thoughts returned to the day he'd ended the two of them. They'd been in love. At least, she had been. It had taken her a long time to accept he'd lied about his feelings.

Over the years, she'd come to understand he'd confused desire with love. It had taken time to forgive him, but she had, placing him in her past.

The way she'd fallen into his embrace, kissed him with years of constrained passion, proved shoving him into her past had been a lie. The man who'd broken her heart still owned it.

Wyatt assembled everyone for herd assignments. He would take point, while everyone else was assigned flank, swing, or drag. At least two ranch hands would be in each position to help those not as familiar with their duties. The ranch's remaining men would stay on drag at the back of the herd. They suffered the worst of the dust while keeping the herd moving.

"If you don't have a bandana, grab one from this bag." Wyatt pointed to a sack at his feet. "Virgil has your assignments. Make sure you pack three bottles of water in your saddlebags, a couple protein bars, and as many apples as you want. There are two pack horses with extra supplies if you run out. We expect to be at the southern pasture in three hours. Once the herd is settled, we'll ride on to the ranch. There'll be plenty of barbecue, drinks, and desserts for everyone. All you volunteers, we appreciate your help."

The riders headed to where Virgil stood off to one side. Lily and Daisy took places at the back of the line, both eating protein bars. Lily felt the jitters in her stomach dance a jig. She hoped to ride near Daisy while praying Virgil would be roving the herd, making certain everyone understood their assignments.

"Ladies." His smile shone bright as the morning sun, and lethal as a wolf. "Daisy, you're riding right swing, and, Lily, you're on left swing."

Daisy tilted her head. "We aren't together?"

"Wyatt thought this would be better. He'll be moving from point to swing after an hour. You'll be with Barrel until Wyatt replaces him."

Stuffing the empty protein bar wrapper in her pocket, Lily lifted her chin. "Any reason I can't ride with Daisy until then?"

"Yes. You'll be riding with me."

Daisy placed a hand on her shoulder. "That's excellent. I'll go find Barrel."

Watching her dash away, Lily knew she'd been thrown under the bus by her best friend. Arguing would be a waste of time. Plus, a part of her wanted to spend more time with him.

There were questions requiring answers. One in particular.

"Appears everyone's ready to go." He grabbed her hand and began walking. Too soon, he let it go, well before she'd figured out what it meant.

Kissing her and holding her hand. What was going through his mind?

"Here you go." Virgil held out Jiminy's reins before swinging into his saddle. "Come on, babe. We're holding up the ride."

Midway through placing her boot in the stirrup, she stopped. Babe? What in the world was happening? Mounting, she glared at him.

"I'm not your babe."

Another smile broke across his face. "If you say so."

Watching him ride away, she felt her anger swell. Not the yelling and screaming kind. This anger grew from confusion and a solid amount of frustration. She hated being in the dark.

Finding her place near the front of the herd on the left side, she put as much distance between her and Virgil as possible. Not easy when he seemed determined to stay close to her.

It wasn't a long ride in miles. They didn't push the herd hard, allowing for a slower trek. It suited the cattle, and definitely suited Virgil as he kept a position within a few yards of Lily.

"You're overthinking something, Lily. Why don't we check a couple items off your list so we can enjoy the barbecue?"

The mooing, bellowing, and snorting of the cattle had lulled her into a sense of peace. His question broke the calm. Uncapping a bottle of water, she took several swallows before shoving it back into her saddlebag.

"There's really just one question of real importance."

"And I'll answer it. Just not now."

"Why?"

His jaw worked as he watched a few of the cattle debating whether to break away or stay with the herd. He sat back in the saddle when they moved back with the others.

"It's complicated. You'll have more questions once I explain the reason behind my actions. We'll need to be alone when we talk about it."

She stared at him, the impact of his statements hitting her in the chest. "I never saw it as complicated. You lost interest in me, wanted to date others when you left for college. I was your past, and you looked forward to your future."

The muscles in his face tightened. "You are so wrong, Lily. I never wanted to end things between us." Drawing a hand down his face, he exhaled a slow breath. "It's so much more complicated than you've imagined."

She'd never thought there were other reasons for their breakup. All these years, she'd been certain he'd lost interest, wanted his freedom when leaving for college.

"Let me answer some of your other questions now. I'll come by to your apartment later tonight and explain what I know."

"All right." How else could she respond? At least she'd get some answers, which was more than she'd ever had. "Tell me about you and Emma."

"There is no me and Emma. I know you've gotten it into your head there's something going on, but you're wrong. It's my fault. I messed up the day you left the ranch after recovering from your accident. As soon as you appeared in the kitchen, I should've ended the conversation with Emma and come to you."

"Why didn't you?"

He thought back on that day, remembering the confusion on Lily's face. "Emma went through a bad breakup with her husband. She'd received a letter from him that morning, begging her to reconcile. I don't know why she chose to share some of her past with me."

"You felt you couldn't leave her to come to me."

He blew out a frustrated breath. "Yes. Then Barrel drove you home, and you wouldn't return my calls. It all spiraled downhill from there. Please understand, Lily. There's nothing between me and Emma."

She thought of all the miserable dates over the last few months. Time she could've spent with Virgil. Pride and her stubborn nature had kept them apart.

Hearing a whoop, they both looked up, surprised to see the large ranch house in the distance.

"You'll stay for the barbecue, right?" His question came out as more a plea.

"Yes. I'll stay. Be warned, though. I do have a few other questions."

His smile warmed her. "Never doubted it."

Chapter Six

Virgil stayed clear of Emma as he and Lily loaded their plates with barbequed brisket and ribs, potato salad, baked beans, salad, and rolls. Taking seats next to Wyatt and Daisy, the four talked among themselves while cleaning their plates.

"How about I get a plate full of desserts?" At their nods, Virgil caught sight of the table laden with pies, brownies, cookies, and what he thought was some kind of chocolate pudding cake thing.

The dessert plates were small, forcing him to heap the sweet confections on top of each other. Juggling two plates and napkins, he began turning away when an older woman blocked his path.

"Excuse me." He moved around her, but not before looking at her face. Something about her slight smile, her eyes, niggled at him. Ignoring a sense of intense unease, he returned to the table.

Sharing what he'd brought, the conversation again turned to the ranch and the changes coming within a few months. Virgil spotted the older woman talking to Anson.

"Wyatt, do you know the woman talking to your father?"

Glancing over his shoulder, he shook his head. "No. She doesn't look familiar."

Curious, Daisy and Lily couldn't stop themselves from taking their own glimpse of the woman.

"Never seen her before." Daisy bit into a brownie, humming in pleasure.

"Me, either." Lily held a cookie in the air. "Except there's something about her eyes that seem familiar." Her gaze moved to Virgil, then back to the woman. Lily's mouth pinched into a tight line when she spotted Jasper joining Anson and the woman. "Uh, Virgil?" She nodded toward the group.

Following her gaze, Virgil's jaw tightened when he saw his father speaking to the woman.

"Do you remember the picture you showed me of you, your father, and mother?"

Instead of answering, Virgil's nostrils flared. Shoving his chair back, he stalked toward his father, and the woman he felt certain was...

"What are you doing here?" The venom in his voice surprised those talking, including him.

"Virgil!" His father's reprimand had no effect.

"What? It's been twenty-three years. We've done fine without her." Virgil studied the woman a moment before coming to a conclusion. "She doesn't belong here." Whirling around, he stalked toward the barn, disappearing inside.

Wyatt had watched the interaction, stunned at the bitterness on his best friend's face. "Excuse me, ladies."

Rushing after Virgil, he ducked into the barn, finding him tossing buckets, old rope, and tack in every direction. Muttering to himself, he didn't hear Wyatt approach.

"Hey, Virg. What's going on?"

When Virgil didn't answer, he stepped in front of him. "Who is the woman?"

Blowing out a heated breath, he straightened, working to get his uncharacteristic anger under control. Ignoring the splintering sensation in his chest, he met Wyatt's gaze.

"Twenty-three years and she shows up as if she belongs here."

Eyes wide, Wyatt said nothing, fearing he knew who Virgil spoke about.

"The woman talking to your father and mine? She's my mother."

Daisy watched the woman stare at the barn where Virgil and Wyatt disappeared. "Do you know who she is, Lily?"

"I can't be sure, but she looks a lot like the woman I saw in a picture with Virgil and Jasper." She glanced at Daisy. "If it's her, then we're looking at Virgil's mother."

"After all these years, she just shows up?"

"It appears so." When Lily went to stand, Daisy reached out to grip her arm.

"Give Wyatt and Virgil a few minutes."

Daisy was right, but it was hard sitting here, wondering about the woman. In all the years she'd known Virgil, she'd never seen him so angry. It was a rare occurrence when he showed any amount of temper.

"Jasper doesn't seem at all surprised about her being here, does he?"

Daisy watched the couple talk, confused at the smile on Jasper's face. "No. Makes me wonder if he knew she was coming to the ranch."

"Why wouldn't he tell Virgil in advance? Blindsiding him wasn't a good way for him to see his mother after so long." Lily wrapped her arms around her waist. "I feel horrible for him."

"There they are." Daisy nodded at the barn.

The two men walked straight to Wyatt's truck. A moment later, they drove away, heading in the opposite direction of town.

Lily slowly stood. "Where are they going?"

"Daisy?" Both looked up at Barrel's voice. Striding up to them, he shoved both hands into his pockets. "Wyatt asked me to tell you he and Virgil are going for a ride. Said they'll be back in a while, and not to worry."

"I guess it would be best for me to drive back to town. It could be hours before they return." Lily picked up used plates and cups, tossing them in a nearby trash can.

"You don't have to run off. Don't you want to meet his mother?"

"It doesn't seem right until I speak with Virgil."

47

Daisy's excitement faded. "I suppose that's true. I'll wait for Wyatt to return before introducing myself."

"Can I help clean up before leaving?"

"We've got plenty of people to help, Lily. Are you sure you don't want to stay a while longer? We haven't had much chance to talk."

"I don't work tomorrow. If you're going to your shop, we could meet for coffee or for lunch when your helper arrives." Lily hadn't shared her decision to leave Brilliance.

After today's ride with Virgil, her plans were on hold until he finished his explanation about leaving her. He'd planned to stop by her place later tonight. She wondered if the arrival of his mother would change his plans.

"Let's meet for lunch at the deli close to your apartment. I want to see what you've done to it."

Lily shrugged. "Not much has changed since you helped me move in. A few more books, a couple plants. If you want, we'll get sandwiches and eat at the apartment."

"Perfect. I'll meet you at the deli at noon." Hugging Lily, Daisy stepped away. "I'll call you when Wyatt and Virgil get back."

Climbing into her car, Lily took one more look at Virgil's mother. She had her arm through Jasper's, as if they'd never been apart.

Lily had decided not to share her interest in leaving Brilliance with her best friend. She wouldn't mention it to anyone until she knew more about Virgil's intentions.

Before leaving, Daisy had confirmed the woman at the barbecue was indeed Virgil's mother. As far as she knew, the woman had been silent about her reason for her visit.

She didn't worry about not hearing more from Virgil, knowing he'd be coming by in a few hours. After eight years, he would explain why he had to break up with her all those years ago. The words 'had to' kept playing across her mind. As if he'd been forced.

Trying not to check the time again, she adjusted the heat in the room. Pulling her phone from a pocket, she let out a slow breath. Seven-thirty, and still no calls or texts. She'd expected to hear from him by now. Debating, she sent him a text. An hour later, he hadn't responded.

At nine, she decided he wasn't going to come by, believing his absence had to do with the appearance of his mother. Her freezer held two types of ice cream. Dipping into both containers, she filled a bowl with chocolate caramel fudge and buttered pecan. She didn't try to find a comfortable spot in the living room, preferring to sit alone at the small kitchen table.

She told herself he'd been held up at the ranch, or there'd been an issue with his mother. Several excuses ran through her mind, none precluding him from contacting her.

Lily gave up at eleven without a word from him. She didn't understand why she'd expected him to show, or why his nonappearance disappointed her so much.

She blamed the kiss.

He'd blindsided her with their side trip, the sweet way he'd shown her the eagle's nest. His explanation about Emma had satisfied her curiosity. Staring at the ceiling from her place in bed, she wondered if he'd lied about his attraction to the lovely cook. Lily didn't believe so.

Which meant he simply hadn't thought about her, had forgotten his offer to bring dinner. Or he'd changed his mind about explaining his actions years ago.

Virgil had struggled with what to do ever since seeing his mother so cozy with his father. The sight had made his stomach twist.

Jasper had just looked at him when Virgil questioned his actions. He'd refused to provide an explanation of why she'd shown up after years of being absent. Virgil concluded his father had known she'd be at the barbecue. He might have even invited her. It would've been nice if he'd shared the information with his son.

Sickened and angry, Virgil packed all his belongings, leaving the small apartment he'd shared with his father at the back of the bunkhouse. Jasper had said little as he watched his son stuff all he owned into two duffle bags.

Virgil hadn't decided where he'd go as he loaded Migisi into the horse trailer. He didn't feel bad about it belonging to his father, or not telling anyone of his decision to leave. A text to Wyatt would be enough.

He'd requested a long overdue vacation. A few days, a week at most. His best friend had understood.

Remembering a campground with a trailhead south of Brilliance, he steered the truck through town. Reaching out to change the radio channel, his arm froze midair.

He spotted Lily's apartment up ahead. His promise to stop by tonight came rushing back to him. Pulling back his arm, he gripped the steering wheel with both hands.

Just because he left the ranch for a few days to cool off didn't mean he had to stay away from Lily. He could do whatever he wanted, see anyone he pleased.

Virgil owed her an apology, and an explanation. The last made him grimace. It had taken him a long time to come to terms with Jasper's demand he break up with Lily. He had no idea how long it would take her to accept his explanation.

The campground where he planned to stay was a few miles south of town. Most spaces filled rapidly in the summer and early fall. During spring, when the weather still held a chill and the streams were frigid, the likelihood of finding a site were higher.

Plus, this was a campground for riders. Spots had an extra place for a horse trailer. Small, round troughs were placed at each site with flakes of hay available for a fee.

Virgil didn't worry too much about feeding Migisi. He'd loaded hay and a large sack of grain in the back of his truck. Tomorrow, he'd buy apples at the store, and food for himself.

Spotting the turn to the campground, he slowed, then stopped. She might be angry, not want to see him again, yet he had to get a message to Lily.

Chapter Seven

Lily grabbed her pillow, flipping it to cover her ears. She'd had a dream. An exceptional dream which included Virgil. Something kept interfering until she gave up the dream.

Loud pounding on the front door startled her, a frown creasing the spot between her eyes. Disgruntled, she grabbed a sweater to cover her pajama pants and tank, and plodded out of her room.

Walking past the kitchen, she groaned at the time. Seven o'clock on her day off.

The pounding began again. "I'm coming!" Someone was impatient, she thought, taking a look through the peephole. *Virgil.*

"Open the door, Lily. I brought a peace offering."

She looked through the peephole, seeing a pink and white bag from the bakery. Then she spotted the cups of coffee.

"Just a minute." Running to her bedroom, she slipped out of the sheer sweater, grabbing a hoodie which matched her pajama pants. Rushing back to the door, she drew it open, not offering a smile. "Good morning, Virgil."

"Hope I didn't wake you."

Ignoring the comment, she nodded at the sack and cups. "Would you like to come inside?"

A small smile tipped up the corners of his mouth. "That would be best, unless you'd rather I turn around and take all this with me."

Reaching out, she took the carrier with two cups from him, knowing he'd follow her to the kitchen. "I'll get napkins. Do you want cream or sugar?"

"Nope. I already fixed up both drinks before leaving the bakery." Tugging one from the holder, he set the large cup at her place before retrieving his. "Decaf caramel macchiato with extra whip. Right?"

Raising a brow, she joined him at the table, handing him a napkin. "Right. But don't be offended if I need more sugar."

"Not a problem." He tossed extra packets of sugar on the table. "I came prepared."

Fighting a chuckle, she took a sip, humming at the taste. "Perfect."

A self-satisfied grin split Virgil's face before he swallowed some of his own coffee.

"Let me guess. Black with a couple dollops of cream and one sugar." She set her cup down before reaching for the bag. Looking inside, her stomach rumbled. "A cinnamon bun. I haven't had one of these in...well, I don't know."

"That one's mine." He held up his cup to cover his grin.

"What?" Face falling, her mouth twisted in disappointment.

"Kidding, Lily. It's for you. The coffee cake is for me."

Grabbing two plates, knife, and two forks, she set out both pastries. "How about we share?"

"Sharing is fine with me." He'd share anything, at any time, with Lily.

They ate in silence until every crumb was gone and their coffees were halfway gone. Leaning back in his chair, Virgil stretched out his legs, crossing them at the ankles.

Lily noted his relaxed pose, which warred with the tension in the room. She wondered who would speak first about him standing her up the night before. Focusing on his face, for the first time since he'd arrived, she saw new lines around his eyes and mouth. He might be smiling, yet his features told her something serious bothered him.

"You look tired."

Glancing down at his hands, Virgil released a tired breath. "I didn't sleep well."

"Because of your mother?"

Hands fisted on his thighs, he snorted, his features taut. "Haven't seen her since I left the barbecue, and I hope not to before she leaves."

"How do you know she doesn't plan to stay?" She winced, wishing she'd stayed silent.

"Unless she intends to live at the ranch, I don't care what she does."

Tracing a finger along the edges of her plate, she softened her words. "I don't see how she could expect to stay there. Not unless Wyatt gives her a job."

"Or Anson."

Lily thought of Wyatt's father talking to Virgil's mother, the two acting as if they were old friends. Her understanding was Jasper and Virgil came to Whistle Rock Ranch after his mother left them. When had Anson and Monica Redstar met?

"Has she ever come to the ranch before?"

"Not that I know about." Pulling his legs up, he straightened in the chair. "After seeing her yesterday, it appears there may be a lot I don't know."

Standing, Lily picked up their empty plates and forks, setting them in the sink. Turning to face him, she leaned against the counter. Virgil wasn't paying attention to her, giving Lily a chance to observe him.

He didn't often come to town during the week. His appearance at her place now made little sense, other than his need to make amends for the night before.

"Shouldn't you be at the ranch?"

"I'm taking some time off."

If they hadn't been friends long ago, she would've thought he was teasing. The set of his jaw, the scrape of his voice, said as much as his words.

"Why now?"

"I'm certain you can guess."

Shoving away from the counter, she returned to the table. "You left because your mother showed up. What will you do if she stays?"

"Deal with it. I'm taking a few days to get my mind around her being here. Twenty-three years without a word, and the woman struts around as if she belongs. Worse, I'm certain Dad knew she was coming."

"Jasper knew and he didn't tell you?"

"Yep."

Leaning forward, she rested her arms on the table, her mind spinning. Jasper never kept secrets from his son. Not unless ordered to by Anson. "He told you he knew?"

"No, but I could see it in his eyes, hear it in what he didn't say. I believe they've been communicating for a while." His hand slapped the table, startling her. "How could he do that, Lily? Bring her to the ranch without warning me?"

The pain in his voice pierced her heart. "Where are you staying?"

"At the campground a few miles south of town. It allows horses."

A tiny grin appeared. "You brought Migisi?"

"Couldn't leave her behind when I don't know how long I'll be gone."

Her phone rang before she could respond. Seeing the face of a longtime friend, she decided to take the call. "Give me a minute, Virgil." Walking into the living room, she answered. "Good morning, Braydon. How's your mother?"

His mother had been fighting terminal cancer, already beating the odds by several months. "Not good. She's, uh, failing real fast."

"Where are you, Bray?"

"At my house. Mom has been here since moving into hospice care. The nurse who's been visiting spoke with the oncologist. The doctor told her to...he said to..."

She heard his sob, her heart breaking. "I'm on my way. I'll call Daisy. Who else do you want there?"

"No one else," he choked out. "Thanks, Lily."

"You just stay with your mother. I'll be there in fifteen minutes." Hanging up, she saw Virgil standing a few feet away. "You know Bray Stiles?"

He nodded. "Heard his mom's been fighting cancer."

"Seems her fight may be almost over."

"Get dressed. I'll drive us over while you call Daisy."

"You don't—"

"Go on and dress, Lily. Bray will accept all the support offered."

Braydon hadn't exaggerated when telling Lily his mother had little time left. Within an hour of arriving, the woman who'd supported her son by working long hours without complaint, took her last breath.

Knowing her death was coming didn't make a difference to Braydon. His sobs were quiet, yet soul deep. With no siblings or other relatives, Daisy and Lily offered whatever support they could, which included communicating her death and handling funeral arrangements.

A successful financial planner, Braydon had a hard time making the simplest decisions. He had no close friends. His entire life had focused on helping his mother put food on the table and saving enough to attend college.

When attendants from the funeral home arrived, Virgil placed a hand on Braydon's shoulder. "Come on. Let's go outside and get some air."

He scrubbed a hand over his face, making no move to leave. "I don't know if I should leave."

"It would be best to let us do our job, Mr. Stiles." The older of the two attendants spoke in a quiet, respectful voice. "Getting out of here for a while might help."

Giving a slow nod, Braydon took his time leaving the bedroom, his movements those of an elderly man. Staying close, Virgil led him to the professionally landscaped back yard. They headed to a gazebo with built-in benches covered with custom made cushions.

"I had this installed because Mother loved being outside. When she could no longer walk, I had the contractor build a ramp for the wheelchair. I'd bring out my laptop and work while she enjoyed the spring sunshine." Removing his glasses, he pressed his palms against his eyes. "Maybe I'll have it torn down." Lowering himself onto a bench, he clasped his hands in his lap.

Sitting beside him, Virgil glanced around the beautiful backyard. "Don't make any decisions for a few months, Bray. Seems to me the gazebo will be a wonderful reminder of your mother and her joy of being outside."

Rocking, he stared at his joined hands. "You think so?"

"I do. What causes you pain today may be the source of great pleasure once your grief subsides. Someday, when you're married and have children, you can tell them all about their grandmother and how she loved the gazebo."

"She's all I had."

"Not true. You have many friends in town, such as Daisy, Lily, and me. Wyatt is also a friend, as is his mother, Margie. Sometimes, we get so busy making a living, we forget what's right in front of us."

The sound of the side gate opening drew their attention. A young woman entered the backyard, hurrying toward them. Nodding at Virgil, she stopped in front of Braydon.

"I just heard about your mother from Lily. How can I help?"

Slowly rising, Braydon looked down at the lovely neighbor from his mother's neighborhood. Wrapping their arms around each other, he rested his chin on the top of her head.

"Ah, April. You've helped by just being here."

Chapter Eight

Monica Redstar walked the perimeter of the large ranch house before taking a path to the barn. Most of the ranch hands were taking care of the horses or cattle, a few working in nearby corrals. Nowhere did she see Virgil.

Not surprising, as she knew he'd left the ranch the evening of the cattle drive, taking his horse with him. It hurt, knowing her son hated her so much he couldn't stand to look at her. Not that she blamed him.

Walking out on Virgil and Jasper had been the worst single decision of her life. She could make any number of excuses. None of them would soothe the pain of a boy who'd been five when losing his mother.

"Can I help you, ma'am?" One of the ranch hands she'd met at the barbecue walked toward her, a coiled rope in one hand.

"I'm looking for Jasper."

"Last I heard, he returned to his apartment at the back of the bunkhouse to lay down. I can check if you need to talk to him."

"Please don't bother him. I'll see him at dinner."

"Well, I'd best get back to work." Touching the brim of his hat, he sauntered off.

Watching him leave, Monica wondered why she'd made the drive from South Dakota. The answer hadn't changed since she and Jasper had started communicating months earlier.

Continuing along a path around the barn, she recalled her first letter to him. It had taken her five tries before coming up with something worthy to mail. Another week passed before she had the courage to mail it.

When a month went by without a response, she accepted Jasper had no intention of writing back. The disappointment had been acute.

Wrapping both arms around her waist, she walked on, breathing in the late afternoon air. Clean and pure, with the scent of hay and horse. So different from their home on the reservation in southeast Montana.

Heading into the horse barn, she went to the first stall. A mare lifted its head to look at her with large, soulful eyes. "Aren't you a beautiful girl." Reaching out a hand, Monica let the mare sniff her before stroking the horse's nose.

"She's Margie's. Virgil and Wyatt trained her." Jasper stepped beside her.

Monica's hand stilled before she drew it back to her side. "What's her name?"

"Bella. She's just under fifteen hands. A registered Paint born right here on the ranch."

"A perfect name for her. She truly is beautiful."

Moving around Monica, he walked to the next stall. "This gelding is Mighty Quinn. He belongs to Wyatt."

"Do Wyatt and Virgil train all the horses?"

Facing her, his expression didn't change. "Ninety percent. Like you, those boys were born to work with horses."

Swallowing the gnarled knot of regret, she pursed her lips, offering a slow nod. "I saw Virgil drive off with his horse. Which is her pen?"

He walked the few feet to the stall next to Quinn's. "Migisi is a mare."

Rubbing her forehead, she let out a long sigh. "He hates me."

"His memories of you are tainted by the vision of you leaving us."

Putting distance between them, she shook her head. "I shouldn't have come. It was a bad idea."

"This may be your one chance to get to know your son."

"Not if he refuses to speak with me."

Reaching out to touch her, he changed his mind, letting his arm drop to his side. "Give him time."

Choking out a wistful laugh, she stared at her boots. "I don't know how long I can stay."

"You're welcome to stay as long as it takes. Healing your relationship with Virgil is important."

"Yes, I know." Leaning against a nearby stall, she crossed her arms. "What about healing our relationship? Is there a chance we can do that?"

Jasper's throat constricted, making it difficult to respond. "For now, you should focus on Virgil."

She understood his meaning. Their time together died years ago, and they both were at fault. "Do you know how long he'll be gone?"

"A few days. A week at most."

"Do you know where I can find him?"

Jasper shook his head. "Even if I did, I wouldn't tell you. He needs space, time to accept you've come back. Virgil's no coward. He'll come to you when he's ready."

Neither spoke as she walked to the side door of the barn, looking at the majestic Tetons across the valley. Whistle Rock Ranch encompassed thousands of acres in one of the most beautiful locations in Wyoming. In all her travels, she'd never seen any place quite like it.

"Margie told me they plan to open a dude ranch."

"Wyatt's idea after living with his aunt and uncle during college. They've run a successful dude ranch for several years. Along with his degree, he gained a lot of experience. Wyatt's brothers, Jonah and Gage, will be back at the ranch in a few weeks to help with the operation."

"What about Virgil?"

"He'll continue with breeding and training, and take on the organization of all activities, which include horses and cattle. Trail rides, lessons, cattle drives. All four boys are critical to the success of the new venture."

She shifted to look at him. "Do you believe in it, Jasper?"

"A hundred percent. With those boys involved, there's little chance of it failing."

"What will you do?" Monica knew about him being diagnosed with asthma. Margie had shared how it limited his work around the ranch.

Chuckling, he stared out at the vast landscape. "Wyatt and Virgil want me to be more involved with the dude ranch. That would be a death sentence for an old cowhand like me."

Studying his profile, the strong curve of his jaw, and prominent nose, she knew Jasper could do anything he wanted. "A new adventure for you. Think of all the stories you could tell around a campfire." Her lips tilted in a grin.

"Now you sound like Virgil."

"I'll take that as a compliment."

Turning toward her, his face sobered as he studied her. "You and Virgil are alike in many ways. Proud, stubborn, smart as heck, and two of the best natural horse trainers I've ever known. If you'd stayed..." His voice trailed off, unable to finish. Stalking away, he headed toward the main barn doors. "I'll let you know if I hear from him." Lifting his hand, he gave a slight wave before heading outside.

"What are your plans?" Wyatt reached out to add more wood to the campfire. It had been three days since Virgil left the ranch.

"About my mother, the ranch, or what?" Virgil leaned back, staring up at the clear Wyoming night.

"All of it. You know I'll give you whatever time you need. It's just this might be your only chance to get to know your mother."

"Monica. That woman isn't my mother."

"She and Jasper might disagree with you. Because she left when you were five doesn't mean she wasn't a good mother before then."

He shot Wyatt a side-eye. "You don't know what you're talking about."

"Yeah, I get that. Pop and Mom were always there for me and my brothers. All I'm saying is you don't want to look back twenty years from now and wish you'd given her a chance to explain."

Stretching out his legs, Virgil couldn't argue with Wyatt's logic. He couldn't seem to forgive his mother for leaving them. For leaving him. What kind of mother walked out on her young son? A lousy one was his answer.

"I don't know why she showed up now. After twenty-three years, she suddenly wonders what her kid is up to? Maybe it has nothing to do with me and Jasper. Maybe she's here for money. Or she might be looking for work. Wouldn't that be perfect?" Bending down, he tossed more wood on the fire.

"Could be as simple as wanting to see her son again. She might regret leaving and wants your forgiveness. You won't know until you ask her."

Virgil's chuckle was brittle. "And here I was hoping she'd be gone when I returned to the ranch."

Wyatt stood, walking to the cooler to grab a couple bottles of water. Tossing one to Virgil, he removed the cap, downing half of his.

"Jonah and Gage will be here this weekend. I want you there."

"I'll be there. Are they back for good?"

"Not yet. Two more weeks and they'll load a trailer to come home. Then the real work starts."

Virgil knew the success of the dude ranch would secure the future of Whistle Rock Ranch. Money would come in from cattle operations, breeding, training, and selling horses, and from entertaining visitors who wanted a real western experience.

It may rub some ranchers the wrong way, but Virgil believed it was a smart move. The Bonners had enough land and experienced men to make it all work. Diversification would secure their future.

"Uncle Emmett and Aunt Lucinda will also arrive for a visit this weekend. They aren't opening their dude ranch until late June, about three weeks later than normal. I'm anxious to get their thoughts on the new venture."

A smile curved Virgil's mouth. He liked Wyatt's aunt and uncle. "Have you approved the marketing material?"

"Three weeks ago. The firm Jonah hired takes care of printing, mailing, social media, advertising, and taking reservations. It costs more initially, but it will give us more time to focus on making sure everything is ready for the first group of visitors."

"Are we still offering first year specials?"

"Yeah. We're keeping the costs below those of similar ranches in western Wyoming. We'll still show a profit. I'd better get going before Daisy starts to worry. How about we load Migisi into the trailer and I take her back to the ranch? It'll give you more time with Lily."

"Who says I want more time with her?"

"I've seen how you look at her. You didn't stay more than a few feet away when I met all of you at Bray's house. That's a real sad situation."

Virgil joined Wyatt by his truck. "He has no one except a few friends. Well, there's his neighbor from the old neighborhood. I plan to stay in touch with him, get him out to the ranch."

"Good idea. Daisy said he loves to ride. Bray's thinking about buying a horse. No better time than now to get his mind off his mother."

Deciding to let Wyatt take Migisi back to the ranch, the two took little time getting the trailer hooked up and the mare loaded. As Virgil watched Wyatt drive away, he thought of his friend's comment.

Braydon had spent most of his free time with his mother during her illness. Lily told Virgil they'd had a close relationship. If his life had been different, if his mother had stayed, he and Monica might have been close.

Returning to his spot before the campfire, he sat down, staring at the flames. Could Wyatt be right? Would

Virgil regret missing an opportunity to spend time with his mother, ask why she'd left?

His question was, what would he do about it?

Chapter Nine

Opening the email, Lily read the contents, her eyes growing wide. Valley Hospital in northern Wyoming invited her to interview for an opening in their emergency room.

Excitement gripped her as she read the short message a second time. Closing it, she opened a second email, this one from the hospital in Laramie. They, too, had an opening and wanted to speak with her.

Both interviews were to take place through video. Easy enough.

Feeling lighter than she had for days, Lily set her laptop on the kitchen counter, and poured a small amount of wine into a glass before heading to the bedroom. Taking a sip, she moved to the bathroom to start her shower. Undressing, she stepped under the hot spray.

Events over the last week ran through her mind as she applied a generous amount of shampoo to her hair. Massaging her scalp, she ticked through each one, her thoughts stalling on Virgil.

She'd spent more time with him in the last week than she had since returning from college. His presence felt right, comfortable, as it had years ago.

Rinsing, she finished before wrapping one towel around her hair, another around her body. Running a brush through her hair, she again thought of Virgil, and the kiss they shared during the cattle drive. She could still feel his lips on hers, the warmth of his arms encircling her. The memory both soothed and frightened her.

Moving to the bed, she laid down, using an arm to cover her eyes. She didn't understand Virgil's renewed attention. He'd shown some interest over the years, spoken to her at church or when she and Daisy rode at the ranch. Never had he shown up with pastries and coffee.

A knock on her door had her sitting up on a groan. She slipped into a robe on her way to the door. Checking the peephole, she sighed.

Virgil stood outside holding a couple bags. Opening the door a crack, she didn't smile.

"I know you didn't invite me. Still, you have to eat sometime tonight."

Inhaling, she recognized the aroma of the best Italian food south of Jackson Hole. "Is that their lasagna?"

"Plus salad, garlic cheese bread, and tiramisu. Plenty for both of us."

Defenses wavering, she gave in when her stomach rumbled. "Oh, all right. You can get out plates while I dress." Rushing to the bedroom, she closed the door, but not before hearing his soft chuckle.

She joined him several minutes later. He stood at the kitchen counter, the food spread out before him. It looked even better than it smelled.

"You didn't have to bring me dinner."

Walking to her, he slid an arm around her waist, surprising her with a slow, deep kiss. "I wanted to spend time with you. Food is as good an excuse as any."

Out of breath from his kiss, she watched him, wanting to ask what was going on.

"Here you go." He handed her a plate with a large portion of lasagna, salad, and bread.

"Thank you."

He joined her a moment later at the table. Setting down the plate, he leaned down to brush a light kiss over her lips. Settling in his chair, he picked up his fork, scooping up a large bite of lasagna. Chewing, he glanced at her.

"Are you going to eat?"

"Um, yes."

"How is Bray doing?" He grabbed a second piece of garlic cheese bread.

Setting down her fork, she washed down her food with a swallow of water. "I spoke with him today. He sounded much better."

"When are the services?"

"Next Monday. Are you able to attend?"

"Yes. I'll pick you up, if that's all right."

She hadn't expected the offer. "If it's no trouble."

His voice softened. "You're never any trouble, Lily."

Surprised at his reply, she nevertheless accepted it. "All right. I'll be coming home to change. I'll let you know the time."

"How about some dessert?"

While Virgil finished his tiramisu in six bites, she took her time, savoring every bite. "When are you going back to the ranch?"

"Tomorrow. Jonah and Gage are driving in from Laramie for the weekend. We'll be working on the new venture. Wyatt's Aunt Lucinda and Uncle Emmett are also expected."

"Daisy asked if I wanted to ride this weekend. Maybe I'll see Jonah and Gage."

"I'm sure they'd like that."

"Since you brought dinner, I'll do the dishes."

"I'll help. Then maybe you'll invite me to stay for a movie."

Warmth spread through her. She wanted to ask about his sudden interest in her, deciding her question could wait.

"Watching a movie with you sounds wonderful. I'll even let you pick."

Moving to the kitchen, they worked together to clean up. There wasn't much other than loading the dishwasher. As Virgil put the last plate away, his gaze landed on an open email on the laptop.

"I'll be right back. I have Netflix and Amazon Prime if you want to pick a movie." Lily headed to her bedroom, closing the door.

Curiosity claimed him. He knew it was wrong to read Lily's email, yet catching the name of a prominent hospital, he scanned the message. His chest squeezed at what he read. Closing it, his gaze landed on a second open email. It was almost a clone of the first, requesting an interview for a job hours away.

Feeling gut-punched, he moved away from the computer. He could almost feel his heart stall at the implications of the emails. Picking up the controller, he sat down, staring at the screen.

He wondered how long she'd been planning on leaving Brilliance. Daisy had told him Lily loved her nursing job, had made friends with her coworkers, and hoped to become a supervisor within a few years. What had changed?

"Have you selected a movie?" She sat down near Virgil without crowding him. "Virgil?"

"I'm still searching." He needed to concentrate, and stop thinking about Lily leaving town. "There's a good one." The title of an action movie with an ensemble of well-known actors spanned the screen.

"I love that one."

A grin quirked the corners of his mouth. "You do?"

"A lot of women like action movies. A diet of a hundred percent chick flicks can get real boring." She waved her hand in the air. "Go for it."

Selecting it, he grabbed her around the waist, tugging her next to him. "You were much too far away."

Partway through the movie, she'd snuggled against him, her head on his shoulder. Virgil didn't want to move, do anything to disrupt their closeness.

Kissing her forehead, his hand moved up and down her arm. When she lifted her face with an expectant look, his mouth covered hers. Letting her free arm wrap around his neck, he deepened the kiss, thoroughly exploring and tasting her.

When the kiss became too heated, he lifted his head, brushing his lips across her cheek. "I've missed you so much, Lily."

"I..." She couldn't finish, afraid of committing to anything regarding Virgil.

"You don't have to say anything. I know it will take time for you to trust me again." He kissed her again. "I'll do whatever it takes to get you back, to have the future we always planned."

"I don't know, Virgil. It's been such a long time, and I'm afraid."

"I know, baby. So am I. All I'm asking is for you to give us a chance. Can you do that?"

She fell silent, her heart pounding so hard it hurt. "I'll think about it."

"That's all I can ask."

Lily worked the following day, her thoughts consumed with Virgil. She'd been truthful when saying she'd consider a second chance. In reality, she didn't see how a relationship could ever work out.

She hadn't analyzed the depth of her distrust until last night. The fear gripping her when he'd confessed his intentions had been quick and piercing. She could no longer look into his eyes and gauge his honesty.

Lily had hoped there'd be a second chance for years. She'd imagined them discussing what happened, and finding a way to put the past behind them.

As teenagers, they'd kiss before talking of marriage and children. It had been romantic, forever, with a guaranteed happy ever after.

She'd been young and in love back then, expecting romance in everything. As an adult, watching other couples face difficulties which sometimes ended their relationship, she knew happy endings were all too rare.

The day he'd severed ties with her had been the worst of her life. It had taken months to accept Virgil no longer wanted to see her, and her entire senior year for the worst of the pain to end.

Whenever the phone rang or she heard a ping signaling a text, she'd expected it to be Virgil. Attending the University of Wyoming after graduation, she'd spotted him many times on campus, never once approaching him.

Transferring had been a real option, eliminating the chance of ever seeing him. Daisy had talked her into staying. Looking back, completing her studies in Wyoming had been the right decision.

Arriving home, she dropped her purse onto a table, stretching both arms above her head before touching her toes. It had been a long day, yet the time had gone fast.

She found the quick pace of the emergency unit challenging and fulfilling. During nursing school, one of the instructors spoke of his time in the emergency room at a large inner-city hospital. Gunshot wounds and knifings were common, as were gang beatings. Lily didn't expect any of those in Brilliance. What she'd handled today convinced her the change from working on a floor had been the right decision.

Grabbing a bottle of water, she sat down before her computer. Yesterday's two emails remained unanswered. Before she could change her mind, Lily responded to each, indicating her availability for interviews.

Instead of the anticipated relief, her anxiety increased. Did she truly want to leave Brilliance? Perhaps the interviews would give her an answer.

Virgil had been angry when leaving her apartment the night before. She didn't blame him, but the words he wanted her to say wouldn't come. The second chance he sought had hung between them until he'd given her a quick kiss and left.

She had the weekend off. A rare event which happened a few times a year. Her schedule would change in another month. By then, she may have accepted a job hours away. The thought soured her already churning stomach.

Not counting the short cattle drive, it had been a while since she and Daisy had taken a ride around Whistle Rock Ranch. Lily looked forward to their ride the next morning.

Her friend had adjusted with ease to life on the ranch. Daisy's once difficult relationship with Wyatt's father, Anson, had transformed to one of easy friendship and warmth.

Setting out her clothes for the following morning, Lily wondered if she'd even see Virgil. He'd mentioned being in meetings most of the weekend. She understood. The four men behind the new venture would be hammering out the last details before advertising Whistle Rock Western Adventures.

Eating a light dinner, she took a long shower before climbing under the covers. A wave of anticipation surprised Lily. She didn't know if excitement at the upcoming ride, the possibility of seeing Virgil, or both caused the slight thrill.

Closing her eyes, she prayed for a long, easy sleep. Within minutes, her prayers were answered.

Chapter Ten

Virgil rose after a fitful sleep in one of the Bonner guest cabins. The same cabins they'd be using for visitors within a few weeks.

Returning to the ranch early the previous morning, he'd managed to avoid his mother until dinner. They'd made polite conversation consisting of short sentences, never touching the reason Monica left Virgil and his father.

It helped that Wyatt's brothers, Jonah and Gage, had arrived for the weekend. Their mother, Margie, placed Monica between the two younger brothers, with Virgil across the table, next to his father. Jasper appeared more rested and in better spirits than he had in months. He had to wonder if his father's improvement had anything to do with Monica's presence. Virgil hated to think she had such a positive effect on Jasper.

The conversations around the table centered on the new venture, a topic everyone could contribute to. Even Monica, a woman who'd been at the ranch such a short time, had suggestions.

Virgil stayed quiet, not unusual for him. He'd given his opinions several times over the previous months, worked alongside Wyatt to develop programs visitors would enjoy. The most demanding would be an end of week cattle drive, similar to what they'd done the week before. Those who didn't choose to ride would still participate in the evening barbecue, cowboy poetry, and music.

Partway through dinner, the front door burst open, allowing Emmet and Lucinda Bonner to enter. "Did we miss dinner?" Emmet's question had everyone smiling.

Several minutes later, they were seated, plates filled with food in front of them. Wyatt's uncle and aunt hadn't visited in a couple years, busy with their own successful dude ranch in Montana.

With them present, the group revisited several topics. As the voices merged, Virgil's thoughts turned to Lily and their unrewarding conversation at her apartment.

He didn't know what to do about the pain caused when he'd walked away from her in high school. It seemed such a long time ago, and they were so young. The odds had been against them, the same as with other teenaged couples.

The differences with Virgil and Lily were the reason for his defection and the depth of their feelings for each other. Even now, eight years later, the connection between them remained strong. So did the distrust radiating off Lily.

"You'll get to meet her tomorrow morning, Aunt Lucinda. Lily will be here by eight. Why don't you ride with us?" Daisy glanced at Virgil for a split second before focusing back on Lucinda.

"Maybe I will. It's been a while since I've ridden for pleasure."

"I might join you," Margie added. "You should come with us, Monica."

A small smile appeared on the older woman's face, reminding Virgil of how she looked when he was young. "Are there enough horses?"

Chuckles and outright laughter gave her an answer before Anson spoke. "We raise horses, Monica. All you need to do is pick one."

"Then I'd love to ride along. Jasper, would you help me select the horse?"

"Of course. Although I suspect you're a better judge of riding horses than me." The table quieted at Jasper's comment. "Monica is an excellent trainer."

Anson gave a slow nod. "I do remember you telling me that. If you're looking for work, we're always interested in an experienced trainer. Right, Wyatt?"

Knowing Virgil wouldn't be thrilled to have his mother working on the ranch, he hesitated before replying. "We should talk about your plans, Monica."

"I don't know how long I'll be staying."

Virgil tensed at her answer. "She has a problem sticking." Setting his napkin on the table, he stood. "If you'll excuse me." Walking to the kitchen, he grabbed his hat and coat before stepping outside.

He'd made the decision to not return to the apartment he shared with his father. Roomy, comfortable, and attached to the main bunkhouse, it had been his home the majority of his life. The time had come to build his own place. Until then, he'd stay in one of the cabins.

Stopping several feet from the house, he placed fisted hands on his hips to stare up at the clear night. Sucking in a lungful of air, he let it out, wishing he'd said nothing.

"Virgil. Wait up." Wyatt jogged up next to him, knowing enough to stay quiet, allowing him to work through his rage. The two friends had been through this a few times over the years. Both knew the drill.

"I'll apologize to Margie."

"No need. She understands how you feel. Pop was the one out of line. He should've talked to me before bringing up a job with Monica."

"It doesn't matter. She'll never stay. I expect she'll be on the road within a week."

"What if she doesn't leave this time?"

"There's nothing here for her."

"She and Jasper are getting along pretty well."

Virgil's head whipped toward Wyatt. "What do you mean?"

Lifting one shoulder in a shrug, he looked straight ahead. "You've been gone almost a week. They've spent most of that time together. Maybe there's more going on with her visit than either of them have let on."

Virgil didn't know how he felt about his parents mending their relationship. "Has he spoken to you about them?"

"No, and I haven't asked. I'm telling you what I've seen. They ride almost every day, take meals together in the big house, and go on walks. He took her into town a few days ago."

He let the information settle, his mind whirling with questions. Twenty-three years was a long time for a couple to be apart.

"How's it going with Lily?"

"She's considering taking a job away from Brilliance."

The whinnying of a horse drowned out Wyatt's startled response. "Daisy hasn't said anything about her leaving."

"Maybe she's waiting until there's a firm offer. I was at her place last night and saw two emails requesting interviews."

"I thought she was happy here."

Virgil gave a disheartened sound. "So did I. It's my fault."

"How do you figure?"

Bending down, Virgil picked up a rock, throwing it toward a nearby corral. "I waited too long to get her back."

Wyatt did the same, tossing his rock toward the barn. "You could've waited fifteen years and Lily would still be yours."

"It doesn't happen often, but this time, you're wrong. She's had enough of my inaction. It's one reason she's looking for work elsewhere."

"Daisy's going to have something to say about her leaving."

"You forget Lily doesn't have many close friends. In fact, you, Daisy, and one or two nurses are the extent of her social network. She doesn't get out in the community the way Daisy does."

Adjusting his hat, Wyatt looked over his shoulder at the house. "Lily put a lot of work into the calendar of local ranch women. It was a huge success. They're already putting together one for this year."

Virgil chuckled. "I understand it's going to feature hot cowboys. You should put your name in the hat."

"They've already lined up men for each month. By the way, you're one of them."

The smile on Virgil's face froze. "Not a chance."

"I've seen the list, and you're on it for August."

"No one's spoken to me about being involved. I guarantee this is Daisy's doing."

"I'm not going to argue with you. She's a force. So is Lily once she commits to something."

Virgil thought of the woman he loved, wondering what it would take for her to give them another chance, commit to the love they used to share.

"Is everyone ready?" Margie Bonner twisted in the saddle, seeing four sets of eyes watching her with expectant expressions. Daisy, Lily, Monica, and Lucinda all nodded. "Let's get going."

Lily shot a grin at Daisy, showing her excitement on being back on a horse. Their saddlebags were filled with food, water, and extra clothes. All except Monica had ridden the ranch trails before.

It felt odd meeting Monica after knowing so much about Virgil's past. She'd been prepared to dislike the woman who'd run out on her husband and young son. Although Lily couldn't admit to liking her, she'd made the decision to give her the chance to explain her disappearance to Virgil.

Lily thought of Emma, who hadn't been able to make the ride. The ranch's assistant cook and Virgil had become friends since she and her son arrived. Lily still wondered if their friendship had become more serious than Virgil let on. Deciding it wouldn't matter if she took a job away from Brilliance, she settled into the saddle, determined to enjoy the day and the company.

Margie fell into the lead with ease, while Daisy and Lily took up the rear. They rode a mile before Lily gathered the courage to share what she'd been doing.

"I'm thinking about accepting a job away from here."

Daisy did a double-take before understanding sank in. "You're leaving Brilliance?"

"Considering it. Two hospitals have requested video interviews."

"Why would you leave? You have friends here, a job you love, and, well...Virgil is here."

Shaking her head, Lily chuckled. "He's been home from college for years. Not until the last few months has he made any attempt to spend time with me. All went great right after Thanksgiving, then whatever progress we made fell apart. He's spent a great deal of time with Emma while barely speaking to me since before Christmas."

"I know Christmas was hard on you with Virgil giving presents to Emma and Koa. Still, isn't it worth trying a little longer?"

"No, it isn't. I've wasted more than eight years hoping he'd change his mind about us. *Eight years*, Daisy. I want to fall in love, marry, and have children." She barely stopped her voice from cracking on the last. "There are no men who interest me here. If I'm ever to have a chance at marriage, I'll have to leave."

Pain flashed across Daisy's face, the lines around her eyes and mouth deepening. "You don't believe you can have all those with Virgil?"

Lily stared straight ahead, unsure of how to answer. "There are times he shows an interest in me, then I don't hear from him for weeks. I believe his interest in Emma is deeper than he'll admit."

Daisy reined her mare to a stop, causing Lily to do the same. She lowered her voice so it wouldn't carry to the women ahead of them. "Virgil is not interested in Emma. They're friends, and only friends."

"How do you know? You're in town five or six days a week, while he and Emma are here at the ranch. I guarantee he's spent more time with her in the last six months than with me." Sighing, she glanced away, not wanting to argue with Daisy. "It's time for me to venture out on my own."

"You've been on your own since your parents died, Lily."

"I don't expect you to understand. You have Wyatt and his family, the ranch, and your business. You're beyond happy, and you deserve every second of it. Soon, you'll want to start a family, which would be wonderful."

"Virgil still loves you. I don't understand his hesitancy other than fear of you rejecting him."

Choking out a laugh, Lily watched the women ride up a low hill. "I doubt he's concerned about rejection. It doesn't matter. He's had plenty of time to make a meaningful move. He hasn't. The time has come for me to do something other than wait." She thought of the other night, the kisses they'd shared.

Clucking, her horse moved toward the other riders. She knew Daisy would follow.

Lily realized her last sentence had been a long time coming. A new beginning might be what she needed to pull herself out of the loneliness shrouding her since Daisy's wedding.

A new town, new job, and a fresh start felt right. Staying in Brilliance would offer nothing except what she'd faced for years.

Freeing herself from the emotional ties still binding her to Virgil suddenly felt right. Releasing a deep sigh, a refreshing sense of calm settled around her heart.

Chapter Eleven

Virgil watched out the window of Margie's office, hoping to see the group of women return from their ride. He'd planned to speak with Lily before they left, missing her by a few minutes.

Determined not to lose the opportunity before she drove home, he continued to take quick glances outside while trying to follow the discussion going on with Wyatt, Jonah, and Gage.

"Virgil, what do you think?"

Shifting to look at Wyatt, he cringed. "Sorry, what do I think about what?"

"I'm thinking our Northern Cheyenne's thoughts are on someone else." Gage smiled as he spoke. Virgil's desire to get back with Lily had never been a secret.

Jonah tapped a pen on his pad of paper, not commenting about Lily. "There's been a suggestion for us to open a gift shop for our visitors."

Virgil focused his full attention on the others. "Who do we have to run it?"

Wyatt shot a look at his brothers, not meeting Virgil's keen gaze. "Have you spoken to Jasper about Monica possibly staying at the ranch?"

Body going rigid, his voice changed to one laced with no small amount of irritation. "Are you saying she won't be leaving?"

Wyatt hated blindsiding his best friend on anything. Catching him unawares on a topic regarding Monica felt especially wrong. "That's what Pop told me."

Shoving back in his chair, Virgil scrubbed both hands down his face before looking up. "Why would she want to stay here? She hasn't wanted anything to do with me or Jasper for twenty-three years."

Jonah tapped his pen faster. "I heard she's sick." Three sets of eyes landed on him. Shrugging, he set the pen down. "I overheard Mom and Pop talking with Jasper. From what they said, she's pretty sick."

"With what?" No one missed the doubt in Virgil's voice.

"I don't know." Jonah's mouth twisted. "All I heard was she needed a place to stay where people could keep watch on her. Margie offered one of the guest rooms. She suggested Monica do something involving the dude ranch."

Rubbing fingers over his forehead, Virgil stood. "What else do we need to discuss before lunch?"

Wyatt knew what his friend was thinking. "We can eat whenever we're ready. Maybe you should go find Jasper and get some answers before meeting us in the kitchen."

With a sharp nod, Virgil stalked from the room, knowing where he'd find his father. Jasper Redstar never missed a meal. Since he wasn't in the main house, Virgil expected to find him in his apartment eating leftovers or one of his outrageously delicious sandwiches.

Walking in without knocking, Virgil came to an abrupt stop. Jasper wasn't inside, nor did he smell the aromas of an earlier lunch. Had he missed him in the house's kitchen?

His gaze searched the corrals and open areas as he returned, not spotting Jasper. Halting, he settled fisted hands on his hips, taking one more narrowed look around. That's when he saw the open spot where his father kept his truck.

Jasper hadn't driven off the ranch since before the asthma episode, which sent him to the hospital months earlier. He'd changed his ways, even giving Nacho, the ranch's head cook, or Virgil, his grocery list.

Hearing a whoop, he whirled toward the sound, seeing Koa toss a stick for Trooper to catch. The female golden lab had been found months earlier near the barn, the survivor of a predator attack. The only remaining sign of her injuries was the slightly shorter hair.

"Hey, Koa."

Rushing toward him, the eight year old laughed when Trooper caught him around the legs. "She's being feisty today." Throwing the stick again, Koa laughed when she took off to find it.

"It's good you're here to play with her. I thought a friend from school was coming out to spend the weekend."

"He'll be here this afternoon. He's bringing his dirt bike! We're going to ride around the ranch."

"Yeah? Well, I hope you have someone lined up to watch you guys."

Koa's slight shoulders slumped. "We don't need anyone watching us. Besides, my mom has already told me not to get too far from the main house. I don't know why everyone worries so much about me. I can take care of myself."

Hiding a grin, Virgil placed a broad hand on the boy's shoulder. "I'm sure you can. Even the men ride out in pairs. You never know what could happen."

Eyes cast to the ground, he stared at his boots. "I know." Dropping to one knee, he wrapped his arms around Trooper. "Can we take her with us?"

"That's a real good idea, Koa. Even with Trooper, you have to do what your mom says and not get too far from the house. Be sure to keep the barn in sight. Have you seen Jasper?"

"He drove off a while ago."

"Did he say where?"

"Nope. Got in the truck and left. Maybe Mom knows." The sound of a truck engine caught their attention. "There's Adam!" Koa ran toward the approaching vehicle, jumping up and down when it came to a stop. When the door opened, the two young boys wrapped their arms around each other before running to the back of the truck.

Virgil didn't recognize the driver. Then again, a lot of new people had moved into their area of Wyoming over the last few years. Staying back, he watched as Emma came out of the house to speak with the driver, who'd busied himself lifting the dirt bike from the back of the truck.

"What's going on?" Wyatt stopped next to him, holding out a sandwich for Virgil.

"Thanks. Koa has a friend spending the night. His name's Adam. I don't recognize the guy with him."

"Me either. Too many new people to remember everyone." Taking a bite of his own sandwich, he took his time chewing. "Did you find Jasper?"

"Koa says he drove off a while ago. Probably had a doctor appointment. Strange he didn't say anything to me." Watching the boys as he finished his sandwich, Virgil couldn't help thinking about him and Wyatt when they were Koa's age.

"Remember those old dirt bikes Jasper and Anson fixed up for us?"

"How could I forget. We darned near killed ourselves racing around. Those jumps we built were awesome. I wonder if we still have them."

Virgil thought a moment before his eyes lit up. "Didn't my dad store them in the barn attic?"

"You may be right. We should check before heading back into the house. You know, there's something I've been wanting to talk to you about."

Wiping hands down his jeans, Virgil turned toward him. "Now's as good a time as any."

"You know Daisy and I are building a house."

"Sure. Everyone knows."

Brushing bread crumbs from his shirt, Wyatt's face grew serious. "I spoke with Pop, Jonah, and Gage. There's two hundred acres butted up against our acreage. We're going to deed it to you. You should—" Virgil cut him off before he could finish.

"I'll pay you for it."

"You've already earned it, so don't ruin the joy of our decision."

Throat thick, Virgil stared down at the ground before lifting his gaze to meet Wyatt's. "I don't know what to say."

"Say you'll build your house close to ours."

"I, well..." Glancing away, he waited until his emotions were under control. "I can do that."

Clasping him on the shoulder, Wyatt fell silent.

"Virgil. We're going to put Adam's stuff away before riding the bikes. Do you want to come?"

The bright smile on Koa's face made him wish he could go with them. "Sorry, but Wyatt, Jonah, Gage, and I have another meeting. You're taking Trooper, right?"

"Yep. Mom thinks it's a good idea too."

"Did Adam bring a helmet and gloves?" Wyatt asked.

"And boots," Adam answered.

"And we're taking Trooper." Koa looked up at Wyatt, almost daring him to object.

Swiping a hand over the boy's head, Wyatt gave a brisk nod. "That's a real good idea. How long will you be gone?"

"I told them not more than an hour before checking back in with me." Emma joined them, giving Koa a stern look. "Right?"

"Yep. I have my watch, Mom."

"I have mine too." Adam held up his left arm.

"Good. And you keep the house or barn in your sights."

"Yes, ma'am," Adam answered for both.

"I promised your brother you'd be safe on the ranch, Adam. All right. Get your gear on. Stop in the kitchen before leaving. I packed water and snacks for you." Bending down, Emma brushed a kiss across her son's forehead.

"Mom..." Koa's groan had the adults sharing a grin. "Let's go, Adam."

They watched the boys run off toward the back of the house. Emma's apartment could be entered from either the outside or through a hallway behind the kitchen. The outside entrance worked great for an active boy who often came inside covered in dirt.

"I'll meet you inside." Wyatt walked off, leaving Emma and Virgil to stare after the boys.

"He'll be fine, Emma."

She sent a worried glance at Virgil. "I know. It's just, well..." Emma wasn't ready to tell Virgil of her suspicions Koa's father might be looking for them. "I'm being foolish. He's eight and needs some freedom."

"If it will make you feel better, I can send Barrel or one of the other men with them."

"Thank you, but I'm sure they'll be fine. If they keep the barn in sight, I'll be able to see them from the house. He's almost nine. If his father was still around, they'd be doing stuff like this all the time."

"Where is he?"

"Who knows?" She hoped her words didn't sound bitter. "The rodeo is his life. Don't get me wrong, he loved me and Koa. Just not as much as he cared about riding broncs."

"Is he any good?"

"Very. He makes a good living." Her attention moved to the boys who'd changed and were running toward their bikes. "More than good, Virgil. Boys! Hold on a minute." She offered a wan smile. "I'd better get the water and protein bars I packed for them."

Shoving both hands in his pockets, his gaze moved to the far pasture to see a group of riders. The women were returning.

Chapter Twelve

Lily narrowed her gaze on the ranch house, certain Virgil was the man standing outside the kitchen door. As the women neared the barn, her attention latched onto two small figures riding dirt bikes. She guessed them to be Koa and one of his friends.

She couldn't hold back a smile. Smart, cute, and rambunctious, he brought a breath of fresh air to the ranch. As much as Lily longed to spend time with Virgil, Emma seemed to be the woman to capture his attention. Maybe he loved her, maybe not. Did it matter when he chose to fill his empty time with her?

The other night had been a strange departure from his usual routine. Showing up with dinner surprised and somewhat annoyed her. Why did he have to show an interest now when ignoring her for so long?

Daisy slid to the ground, handing her reins to Barrel. "The men will take care of the horses, Lily. How about we go inside and get some lemonade?"

Lifting her gaze to where Virgil stood, she saw him watching her with a grave intensity. Lily considered sharing her decision to leave Brilliance with him. What would it matter?

He'd had years to explain his actions, request a second chance. They could've been married with a couple children by now. Instead, he'd chosen to ignore her. That alone told her all she needed to know.

Turning her back to him, Lily faced Daisy. "I'm pretty tired. A hot bath and glass of wine sound wonderful."

"You can spend the night."

"I appreciate the offer. Going home would be best tonight."

Slipping an arm through Lily's, Daisy walked to the parking area, stopping by her car. "I wish you weren't so set on leaving." Removing her arm, she glanced over her shoulder at Virgil. "He doesn't look happy at you leaving."

Mouth drawing into a tight line, Lily refused to look at Virgil. "It's time for me to put an end to the waiting. I'll always love him. I'm simply not willing to risk my heart a second time." Placing a hand on her chest, she swallowed hard. "He did stop by the other night with dinner."

"What happened?"

"He wants a second chance."

"That's wonderful."

"Not really. Why should I gamble my love, knowing odds are the outcome will be the same? There's a reason he stopped seeing me. A reason he won't share. A man with secrets is too great a risk."

"You're right. It's just I hate to see you leave because of Virgil. I wish there was another option."

Steeling herself as tears burned the back of her eyes, Lily wished there was too. "I'm going to negotiate for four days on and three off. Both hospitals offer it for employees who've been with them for at least a year." Lifting one shoulder in a shrug, she forced a tiny grin. "Who knows? Maybe one of them will go for it."

"That way, you'll be able to come home. Or I'll visit you. I've got two wonderful employees who are also artists. I'm certain there'd be no problem getting them to cover for me. What will you do with your apartment?"

"I haven't even thought about it. I'll figure it out once I've accepted an offer."

Leaning against Lily's car, Daisy let the reality of her friend leaving sink in. "It could take months to find the right position."

"It could. Or I could find the perfect job by the end of the week. I'd best get going." Wrapping her arms around Daisy, she closed her eyes. "No matter where I am, we won't lose touch."

"Promise?"

"Absolutely."

Lily wondered about her promise on the short drive home. She and Daisy would be no more than six hours apart. Somehow, thinking about it now made it seem longer than when she'd sent out her resumes.

Strapping the seatbelt around her before leaving the ranch, she'd spotted Virgil. Arms crossed, he'd leaned against the side of the house. Lily couldn't remember when he'd looked so dejected. Except perhaps the day he'd told her they were done.

She knew there was more to the breakup than he'd let on. Something important he hadn't been able to share. Back in the day, her mind had conjured up all sorts of scenarios. The main one being he'd met someone else. Thinking on it now, the reason didn't fit.

Daisy was adamant he hadn't dated in college, and only a few times after returning to Brilliance. Each date had been with a different woman. Lily could still feel the stab of jealousy when she and Daisy had entered the steakhouse to see him with a gorgeous redhead.

Gripping the steering wheel, she questioned each of her decisions regarding Virgil. Why had she continued to put herself in a position to be hurt? Why hadn't she left long ago?

Hope could be the path to great joy, or the road to utter devastation. She'd experienced both. At twenty-seven, she no longer wished to go down either path.

Parking in her designated space, she gathered her belongings. Her steps to the front door were labored, boots almost dragging on the old concrete walk.

The sun hadn't yet set, reminding her of the long evening and night ahead. Unlocking the door, she set everything on the dining room table before grabbing the open bottle of wine in the refrigerator and a glass.

Not bothering to change, she slumped onto the sofa, setting the glass and bottle aside. She couldn't get the image of Virgil watching her drive off out of her mind.

He had to know they couldn't change the past and expect a happy ending. Maybe there'd been a chance when she'd returned from college. She'd foolishly believed he'd seek her out to beg a second chance. How wrong she'd been.

Removing her boots, she stretched out on the sofa, unable to waste more time on her failed relationship with Virgil. Maybe someday he'd explain his reasons. Maybe someday horses would jump the rainbow, she chuckled to herself before falling asleep.

Virgil rapped on Jasper's door an hour after sunrise on Sunday morning. He'd been tempted to march to the apartment the evening before and demand his father provide answers to his questions.

Wyatt had been the one to convince him to approach his father with a clear head and calm manner. Knocking a second time, he stepped back when the door drew open. It took one look at his son for Jasper to understand the reason for the visit.

"Come in. Make coffee while I dress."

Doing as his father asked, Virgil let his gaze sweep around the apartment. A vase he'd never noticed sat in the middle of the table, filled with fresh flowers. A framed photograph of Jasper, Monica, and Virgil had been placed on a bookcase. The same photograph his father had vanquished to the bottom drawer of the dresser over twenty years ago. The sight tore at Virgil's stomach.

Pouring two cups of coffee, he set them on the table and took a seat. When Jasper joined him, he leaned back in his chair.

"I'm here for answers."

Taking a slow sip of coffee, Jasper met his son's intense gaze. "About your mother?"

"Yes. And about Lily."

A brow rose on his father's forehead. After a moment, he nodded. "Which shall we talk about first?"

"Monica."

Placing a leathered hand on the table, Jasper expelled a slow breath. "Your mother is sick."

"What is the diagnosis?"

Standing, Jasper retrieved a folder from the dresser. Handing it to Virgil, he lowered himself back into the chair.

"Primary biliary cholangitis," Virgil read aloud, his brows pinching together. "It's an autoimmune disease. It mainly affects women in their fifties." He looked up. "The report says many people are symptom free for years."

"Your mother has one symptom, which prompted her to seek medical advice."

"What is it?"

"Fatigue. They diagnosed her early."

"The information mentions UDCA."

"It's a medication for those diagnosed with primary biliary cholangitis. She's taking it to slow the progression. There's a good chance the symptoms and the disease won't progress." Running a shaky hand down his face, Jasper swallowed another sip of coffee.

Setting the data sheet down, Virgil picked up his cup. "If it's controlled with medication, why does she need to stay here?"

"There is more to your mother coming here than the disease."

"Do you honestly believe Monica would've sought us out if she hadn't been diagnosed?"

Closing his eyes, Jasper remained silent for several minutes before responding in a slow, measured voice. "I don't know. She is here now, and wants our forgiveness."

"How long did the two of you communicate before you invited her to the ranch?"

The question didn't appear to surprise Jasper. "Over eight years."

"Eight years?" Jaw tight, Virgil stomped to the counter, refilling his cup. "Why didn't you tell me?" Before Jasper could answer, Virgil stalked toward him, holding up a hand. "Wait. She is part of the reason you insisted I break up with Lily." Jasper's eyes widened enough for Virgil to know he'd been right. "What did she tell you?"

When his father didn't answer, Virgil squared his shoulders. "I'm not going to leave until you tell me what she said, and why it had the power to tear two people apart."

"Why does it matter now? You've waited eight years to seek the answer. Was Lily not important to you until now?"

The question had Virgil taking a step backward. "She's always been important to me."

"Not enough to seek answers. You accepted my ultimatum eight years ago, and have never once asked the reason. Why now?"

Slow pain crept across Virgil's chest, making it hard to breathe. It was a good question. A fair question. One he had no answer for until now.

"I was a boy then. Now, I am a man. A man knows what his heart wants."

Jasper gave a slow nod. "And yours wants Lily?"

Thumping a fist against his chest, Virgil straightened to his full height.

"Yes."

Chapter Thirteen

"It's been a pleasure showing you through the hospital, Ms. Cardoza. May I answer any questions before taking you back up to the human resources department?"

Lily walked beside the gorgeous emergency room doctor, a little intimidated by all she'd learned. The Sheridan hospital had four times the beds and staff as Brilliance. She already knew the salary range and the average rent in the area. Assuming her numbers were accurate, she'd be able to save twice as much per month as in the past.

"You've been very thorough, doctor. I don't have any questions. If you don't mind me asking, how long have you been here?"

"Four years. I came from a large city emergency center in the Midwest, but I'm from Wyoming. Moving home was the best decision I ever made. I heard you were born in Brilliance."

"True. I attended the University of Wyoming. I don't see myself ever leaving the state."

Leaving the elevator, he escorted her down the hall. "Here you are. I hope to see you again, Ms. Cardoza."

Accepting his extended hand, Lily thanked him before entering the human resources office. Taking a seat, she glanced around an office twice as big as the same department in Brilliance.

She'd already had her interview in Laramie. Comparing salaries and rent, she wouldn't be able to save as much, but she'd be two hours closer to home. *Home.* The thought brought an image of Virgil.

Lily hadn't spoken to him since the night he'd brought dinner to her apartment. The evening had been as unsettling as it had been wonderful. For a few hours, it reminded her of the evenings they spent together in high school. Dinner, movies, and snuggling together until he'd left for the ranch. They'd been young, happy, with their entire futures ahead of them. How could she know her future wouldn't include him?

An hour later, she drove to the motel. Sparse, but clean, she'd rise early the next morning for the trip home.

Her trip to Laramie and this one had gone well. Each job offered similar opportunities, although the hospital in Sheridan provided more options for promotion. Plus, there was the salary difference.

Spotting a steakhouse a block from the motel, she made a quick decision, turning into the parking lot. Her stomach rumbled, a reminder she hadn't eaten lunch.

She found the large dining area already packed. "Do you have a table for one?"

"Sorry, hon. It'll be at least thirty minutes. There's room at the bar." The hostess swept a hand in the direction. "If you hurry, you could get one of the spots. They serve everything on the dining room menu." She handed Lily a paper menu before turning to the next customer in line.

Thanking the hostess, she selected a spot near the center of the bar, with men on either side. One looked familiar, and she realized it was the doctor who'd given her the tour. Dressed in jeans, a plaid shirt, and cowboy hat, he exuded the spirit of Sheridan.

"Is this spot empty?"

Shifting toward her, a smile brightened the man's face. "Please. It's good to see you so soon, Ms. Cardoza."

"Thank you, Doctor Nagle." Settling herself on the padded, leather covered stool with a high wooden back, she faced him.

"Call me Mason."

"And I'm Lily. So, tell me. What's good here?"

"Everything. That's why people arrive early. It's the best steakhouse for miles around." Picking up a beer, he tilted it toward her. "What are you drinking?"

"A beer sounds good to me."

"Dark or light?"

"What you're having is fine."

"Harry. The lady would like an Absaroka IPA."

"Coming up, Doc."

A large, chilled mug appeared before her in less than a minute. "Thank you." Taking a sip, she grinned at Mason. "This tastes great. A local brewery?"

"Friends of mine started it a few years ago. They're sending product as far south as Cheyenne, and north into Montana."

"Well, this truly is good." She glanced down the long bar. "Harry's the only bartender?"

"Another one comes on in ten minutes. There's a third one on Fridays and Saturdays."

"What can I get you, Miss?"

"Gosh, I haven't even looked. What do you recommend?"

Harry snorted. "Steak."

Shooting Harry a tight look, Mason opened a menu. "Everything's good, but the ribeye is the best."

"I'll have a ribeye, medium rare, and a baked potato with everything."

The bartender gave her a mock salute. "Coming right up. Yours should be ready any minute, Mason."

The silence following Harry's departure relaxed her. Lifting her head, she caught sight of the ballgame on the screen above the bar. "Are you a Mariner's fan?"

Mason shook his head. "Don't pass it around, but I root for the Rockies."

Laughing, she lifted her mug. "So do I."

Harry set a plate in front of Mason. "Here you are. Yours should be ready soon, Miss."

Acting as if he planned to wait for her meal to arrive, Lily nodded at his plate. "Please go ahead while it's hot."

Cutting into the ribeye, he ate a few bites before looking at her. "Are you talking to any other hospitals, Lily?"

"One. The hospital in Laramie. Are you familiar with it?"

Drinking a swallow of beer, he set down his fork and knife. "I have friends who work there. One in oncology and another in the cardiology department. Both seem happy, although I haven't spoken with either in a while. Have you been there?"

"Before coming to Sheridan."

"What are your thoughts?"

She waited until Harry set down her plate before answering. "I'm impressed with both hospitals. Sheridan pays a little more, but Laramie is a couple hours closer to Brilliance." Slicing her steak, she chewed a small bite.

"Do you plan to go home often?"

"I honestly don't know."

A few minutes passed while they ate and watched the game. Mason's question about her going home often stayed with Lily, and she found herself seeking an answer. How often did she plan to drive back? Once a month? Every few months? If her goal was to start fresh, meet new people, there'd be no reason to return often.

The bar burst into a combination of cheers and jeers when the Rockies home run tied the game. She paid no attention. Her thoughts were on the real reason she'd be leaving Brilliance.

Virgil.

If he didn't live and work at Whistle Rock Ranch, she wouldn't consider leaving home to seek a new life. Taking a bite of her baked potato, she found herself wondering if the decision to leave was made for the right reasons.

"If you decide to accept the position here in Sheridan, I'll be happy to show you around."

Lily cut another piece of steak, stabbing it with her fork. "If I move here, I'll take you up on your offer."

Lily didn't stop at her apartment when she drove into Brilliance at almost two o'clock in the afternoon. The several hours drive gave her time to sort out her thoughts on the offers. It had been a difficult choice. Both were excellent positions.

At eleven in the morning, she'd pulled off the road to make a call. Lily had made her decision and wanted to lock it in before changing her mind. Unfortunately, her contact in human resources didn't answer. Leaving a message, she slid the phone into a spot on her console, deciding to follow up later in the afternoon.

Driving down the main street, Lily pulled into a parking spot outside Daisy's shop. Telling her best friend would be difficult, though not as hard as the conversation she'd be forced to have with Virgil.

Climbing out of her car, she glanced around at familiar stores owned by friends she'd known most of her life. Brilliance Coffee & Bakery would be closed, as would the breakfast diner a few doors down. Lily made a mental note to stop by both several times before leaving, to say goodbye and fill up on her favorite coffee and sandwiches.

"Hey, stranger. Did you just get back in town?" Daisy stood in her shop's doorway, a tepid smile not quite reaching her eyes.

Grabbing her purse, Lily walked toward her. "I haven't even been home yet."

"Then I'm honored. I got you a coffee from Lydia's about an hour ago. Oh, and a chocolate croissant."

Giving Daisy a hug, she held on a moment longer than normal before pulling away. "You're the best."

"That's what I keep telling Wyatt. Come in and tell me everything."

Lily loved the shop where Daisy had made her dream a reality. A gifted artist, she designed beautiful jewelry from semi-precious stones, and took amazing photographs of life in and around Brilliance.

She'd often design the frames, doing the work herself before hanging them in the gallery. Her enthusiasm for the work of others had been the catalyst for Wind Song. Besides her own work, Daisy featured a wide variety of Wyoming artists.

The shop had been an almost instant success. In addition to her business, Daisy had been the driving force behind the calendar featuring ranch women. Lily had helped, but everyone knew Daisy made it happen. They were partway through completing photographs for next year's calendar featuring local ranch hands. Both believed it would be a bigger success than their first endeavor.

Lily knew she'd miss the monthly events featuring one or two of Daisy's artists. She'd miss her friend's energy, enthusiasm, and unwavering support.

"I warmed it up. Hope it's all right." Daisy placed a cup in front of Lily before cradling her own coffee. "Spill. Tell me everything that happened while you were gone. And don't even think of leaving anything out."

Chapter Fourteen

Virgil hung up, allowing himself a brief sense of relief. Lily had made it back to Brilliance after being gone an entire week. A week which had him driving by her apartment several times.

The caller told him she'd gone straight to Daisy's, which didn't surprise him. They were as tight as Wyatt and him.

Virgil squelched the strong urge to drive into town. Work at the ranch, and the fact he'd yet to learn Jasper's reason for forbidding him from seeing Lily, stopped him. He knew she wouldn't settle for anything less than the truth, which he'd give her as soon as Jasper came clean.

The day his father gave him the diagnosis for Monica, Jasper had been ready to explain. As they settled in, there'd been a knock on the door. Monica walked in as if she'd been visiting Jasper for years. Maybe she had.

Virgil no longer understood anything about his mother and father. He didn't know where he stood with either. Didn't know where they stood with each other.

After twenty-three years, he felt disconnected, no longer certain if he held a solid place in Jasper's life. What he did know was he wanted nothing to do with Monica.

He felt bad about her diagnosis and hoped the disease wouldn't progress. But it wasn't cancer or heart disease, where all manner of treatments could be prescribed without success. They'd discovered the cause of her fatigue early, prescribing medication.

Virgil didn't know if he could ever forgive her for leaving. He hadn't forgotten the tears streaming down his face, hands fisted at his sides, or his screams for her to come back. At five, watching his mother drive away without a backward glance could never be undone.

At twenty-eight, he wanted an explanation for her leaving. Not from her. Nope. He wanted to hear it from Jasper.

Shoving the phone away, he grabbed gloves from his back pocket and slipped them on. He and Barrel had been working on a section of broken fence since lunch. Virgil estimated three more hours before finishing their work. Three more hours of his mind circling around Lily and her decision to leave Brilliance.

A low growl pulled Virgil from his thoughts of Lily, and Barrel from their work. Straightening, both men took slow steps toward their truck and Virgil's rifle.

"What's a wolf doing out here in the middle of the day?" Barrel muttered as they continued moving. "Something's not right with that animal."

Virgil agreed. The animal's wild eyes and lack of fear at facing two humans wasn't normal. "I think he's rabid. Get in the truck, Barrel."

Reaching for the rifle laying on the open tailgate, he slowly raised it to his shoulder. As he did, the wolf took several menacing steps forward. Lips pulled back in another hideous growl, Virgil spotted telltale patches of foam around the animal's mouth, confirming Virgil's suspicion.

Sensing movement beside him, he moved his head enough to spot Barrel beside him, his own rifle leveled at the wolf. "We don't have much time."

Virgil hated killing any animal, even those posing a direct threat to him or others. The wolf before them couldn't be cured. Feral and sick, he'd most likely attack other humans before succumbing to the disease.

"On my count." He got no further. The wolf came straight at them, giving neither man a choice.

The crack of two rifle shots tore through the still air. Both hit their target, stopping the animal ten feet from them.

Virgil felt sick, while also knowing he and Barrel had no choice but to put down the sick animal. During his life on the ranch, this was the first time he'd been forced to kill an attacking wolf.

"We'd better get him wrapped up. The Game Warden's going to want to have him checked."

Taking a few steps closer to the dead animal, Virgil glanced behind him at Barrel. "You're right. Go ahead and make the call. We don't have anything in the truck to cover him with. Best let the authorities handle the body. They'll want to determine if he has rabies."

"It's pretty obvious, but you're right." Turning away, Barrel made the call.

Keeping a decent distance, Virgil walked around the wolf, a pinch of regret lodging in his chest. He'd been a beautiful animal at one point. Regal even. There was little that could be done once a wild animal was infected with rabies.

"We're in luck. Austin Crane will be out within the hour. He's already close to Brilliance." Barrel joined Virgil near the dead wolf. "A shame, but it couldn't be helped. He was coming right at us."

Offering a slow nod, Virgil turned back to the truck. "We might as well work on the fence until Austin arrives. We'll need to keep watch, as the wolf may draw attention from scavengers. Remind me to put a tarp in my truck."

"You got it, boss."

Virgil took an extra long shower that evening, and ate a quick dinner before driving into town. Parking on the street near Lily's apartment, he stared at the lit front windows. He didn't know if his idea to stop by would result in her turning him away, or an invitation to join her inside.

Several minutes passed before his boots hit the asphalt. Even then, he hesitated. Did he truly want to hear she'd be leaving Brilliance, and him, behind? The honest answer was no.

Forcing himself to move, he closed the distance to her door and knocked. It opened within a few seconds, a surprised Lily standing inside.

Stomach churning, she hesitated a moment while gathering her thoughts. She'd planned to face him sometime, just not the evening of her return.

"Virgil. I didn't expect to see you tonight. Come in."

Stepping aside, she felt a sharp pang of something she couldn't quite define. Regret? Excitement? Disappointment? Desire? The last had her closing the door to wrap her arms around her waist.

"How about something to drink?"

"Water would be great. Thanks." Following her to the kitchen, he leaned against the counter.

"Here you go." Handing him a bottle, she opened one for herself. "How've you been?" Heading to the living room, Lily sat down at one end of the sofa.

Taking a seat at the other end, he took a long draw of water. "Busy. Announcements about the new venture were sent out. Inquiries and reservations are going to Margie for now. We opened up the first three weeks, and they're already booked."

"That's wonderful. You must be excited."

"I'm not sure excited is the right word. It's common to lose money the first season. The Bonner boys are hoping we'll buck the trend and show at least a small profit."

Crossing her legs Indian style, she leaned toward him. "What do you think?"

"I'm leaving the numbers up to them. All I need is a schedule of trail rides and the number of people."

Listening to him, she was struck by a pang of nostalgia. Why had it taken him years to try to rebuild their friendship? And why now, when she'd made up her mind to leave? Hearing his voice, she forced herself to concentrate.

"We'll be offering a ranch rodeo at some point. Wyatt's thinking once or twice during the season."

"Aren't those a lot of work?"

"They are. We'd need men and women from surrounding ranches to participate, and would open invitations to locals, as well as those staying at Whistle Rock."

"I'd love to..." Lily's voice trailed off, remembering she wouldn't be living in Brilliance.

Sensing what she was about to say, Virgil speared her with a probing look. "Tell me about your time away."

Adjusting herself on the sofa, she steeled herself for the conversation ahead of them. "I've been considering jobs outside of Brilliance."

Saying nothing, he waited for her to continue.

Narrowing her gaze on him, she clasped her hands in her lap. "Had you already heard?"

"I saw the emails the night I brought the Italian food."

Face flushing, she glared at him. "You read my email?"

"Both were open on your computer. The hospital logos were hard to ignore, Lily. I would've said something that night, but we had other things to discuss."

Like the fact Virgil wanted a second chance, Lily thought. A request which went unanswered.

The anger, which flared a moment earlier, dissolved at his uneasy expression. "I met with administrators and doctors at two hospitals."

"I see."

"Both offered me a position in their ER."

Leaning forward, he rested his arms on his thighs, staring at the floor.

"The salaries are quite a bit higher, and rent is a little more than here."

Without meeting her gaze, he gave a slow nod.

"One is in Laramie, the other in Sheridan."

"I see."

"The one in Sheridan appeals to me a little more."

Clearing his throat, he stood, walking to the window to look out. "You're moving six hours north?"

"I'm considering it. I left a message asking to speak with them, but I haven't heard back."

Resting a hand against the window, his head lowered to stare at the floor. "I waited too long."

"What?"

"I should've tried to work things out between us earlier. But..."

"But?"

He couldn't share a reason he didn't yet know. "Jasper gave me the ultimatum. I argued, wanted to know why. He never offered an explanation."

"He knew you'd do what he asked," she whispered.

Returning to the sofa, he sat down, covering her hand with his. "There was no asking, Lily. He threatened to disown me."

Straightening, eyes wide in confusion, she tightened her hold on his hand. "Jasper would never have disowned you."

"Don't be so sure. When I refused, he grabbed my shoulders and shoved me to the ground. The look in his eyes reminded me of a wild animal. He knew I'd never lift a hand against him. I've never seen him so panicked."

"What would've caused such a reaction?"

Lifting her hand, he kissed each knuckle before lowering their joined hands to his lap. "I don't know. I've asked him more than once over the years. His reaction was the same as when we were in high school. Whatever the reason, he has refused to tell me."

Scooting next to him, she picked at the edges of her cotton shirt. "What are your plans?"

Placing an arm over her shoulders, he kissed her forehead. "I'm not a teenager any longer. I've let it go out of respect for my father." Tugging her closer, he rested his chin on top of her head. "I can no longer blindly accept his ultimatum. I love you, Lily. I don't want you to leave Brilliance."

"It's too late, Virgil."

"I can't accept that. If we still love each other, there's always a chance."

When she didn't respond, he lifted her chin with a finger. "Do you still love me, Lily?'

Closing her eyes, she considered lying. It wasn't about love. The issue was trust.

"I've always loved you. There comes a time when love isn't enough. A relationship takes trust."

"You don't believe you can trust me."

She shook her head. "I'm sorry, Virgil."

Stroking a hand over her arm, he let out a deep sigh. "Then I'll spend the rest of my life proving you can."

Chapter Fifteen

Lily woke gradually, feeling an odd sense of peace. Her eyes tore open at the feel of hot breath on the back of her neck, strong arms banded around her. Finding herself staring at the living room window, recollection of the night before returned.

She'd been talking with Virgil about the job offers. He'd wanted a second chance, pleaded with her not to leave. They'd fallen into silence when he'd selected a slow moving video, and apparently fallen asleep.

It felt good, and more right than she would've imagined to wake up next to him. Nothing had happened, yet she hadn't experienced such peace in a long time.

A kiss to her neck signaled Virgil was awake. "You smell good," he whispered, sending shivers through her.

"I suppose it's time to get up." Still, she didn't move.

"You're right. Wyatt's going to wonder where I am." Placing one more kiss against her neck, he pulled his arms free and sat up. "Did you sleep well?"

A rueful smile curved her lips as she pushed herself up. "Best in a long time. You?"

"Same."

Their eyes locked for several seconds before Lily stood. "I'll make coffee."

Rising, Virgil reached his hands toward the ceiling, stretching his back. "Have you heard of primary biliary cholangitis?"

Setting two cups on the counter, she cocked her head. "I believe it's a disease of the liver. Why?"

"Monica's been diagnosed with it."

"She didn't seem ill during the trail ride."

"According to my father, her only symptom is fatigue. I'm pretty certain that's why she came to the ranch."

"To be close to you and Jasper?"

"Jasper. I doubt she cares one way or another about me being here. It appears she'll be staying around for a while. Maybe forever." Bitterness coated his tongue, a ball of disgust lodging in his chest.

Placing a cup in front of him, Lily sat down at the table, opening her laptop. "Let's see. Primary biliary cholangitis."

Virgil pulled a chair next to her, reading the search results. "Open the one on top."

"It's an autoimmune disease of the liver," Lily read aloud. "The bile ducts become damaged. It mainly affects women in their fifties." She glanced at Virgil. "How old is Monica?"

"Fifty-four or five. The same as my father."

"Do you know if she's been prescribed medication?"

"According to Jasper, she's taking something."

"Probably UDCA." She pointed to the section of the article describing the drug.

"That sounds right. It's suppose to slow the progression of the disease."

Sitting back in the chair, Lily placed her hand on his arm. "She's been diagnosed early. Does she already have a local doctor?"

"I don't know."

She considered her next question, tossing it aside before deciding to ask. "Do you want me to speak with her? We got along well during the trail ride. Maybe she'll share information she won't with Jasper."

"I appreciate the offer, but I can't ask you to get in the middle of my family problems. At least not until I've spoken with her. Maybe after that?"

"Whatever you need. I'm here for you, Virgil."

Studying her face, his gaze locked on emerald green eyes. "Are you, Lily? Here for me?"

She knew what he meant. Would she be here for him, or take a job hours away from Brilliance?

"For as long as I'm here."

Lily's response stayed with Virgil on the drive back to the ranch, and during his time in the large arena training a young Paint gelding. There'd been no commitment to stay in Brilliance. Changing her mind would take time. Trust, once lost, was almost impossible to recover. The knowledge wouldn't stop him from trying.

"Virgil!"

He turned at Wyatt's familiar voice. "I thought you were meeting with your attorney today."

"Already done. I've got some papers for you to sign. They're in the house when you're ready."

Walking the gelding to its stall, he ran the curry comb over him. "Papers for what?"

"Your two hundred acres."

Virgil straightened, tossing the curry comb into the grooming bag. "You're certain about this?"

"More than certain. You've earned every acre. It's good land, and a great location. You'll be able to graze your horses on Whistle Rock land, so two hundred should be plenty. Of course, you'll have to put up with me and Daisy owning the parcel next to yours."

"Does Jasper know about this?"

"He does. Pop spoke to him before making the final decision."

His own two hundred acres. Virgil dreamed of saving enough to buy his own place not far from the ranch. He'd never considered the Bonners giving him the property.

"When you're finished, come up to the house and we'll get it all settled. One more thing. A man stopped by late yesterday about the job. Says he has plenty of experience. I didn't speak to him long. Told him to come back later today or tomorrow to meet with you."

"Sounds good. I'll watch for him. He got a name?"

"I was in a hurry and didn't ask. Don't worry about me talking to him. If he's solid and you think he'll fit, hire him."

With the first three weeks of the dude ranch filled, they needed a ranch hand good with horses and people. He sure hoped the man worked out.

Finishing, he put the grooming bag away and washed his hands before walking to the house. Excitement coursed through him. His own land next to his best friend. What could be better?

He knew the answer. Lily being with him when he rode the two hundred acres for the first time as the owner.

Giving a quick nod to Emma and Nacho, who worked side by side in the kitchen, he grabbed a bottle of water before crossing the living room to Anson's office. Opening the door, he was surprised to see his father, Anson, Margie, and Wyatt waiting. Taking a seat next to Jasper, he opened the water, taking a long swallow while trying to calm his raging anticipation.

Anson sat back in the big leather chair worn from use, his large hands resting on the desk. "Wyatt told you what this is about?"

"He did. It's more than I ever imagined." Virgil looked at each one. "I don't know how to thank you."

Anson held up a hand. "No need. It's well deserved. You can start building whenever you're ready. Jasper already called a witcher to locate a good spot to drill a well. Might as well get that done soon. Wyatt's going to use the same man."

Casting a knowing look at his friend, Virgil nodded at Margie. "Thank you."

Lifting a shoulder, her lips tipped up in a grin. "Costs less to have him come out one time."

"Read these over, and if all looks good, sign. We'll get it recorded."

Doing as Anson said, Virgil took his time. When satisfied, he signed, sliding the document back across the desk.

Slapping his hands on the desk, Anson stood. "All right. We'll leave you and Jasper alone."

Virgil shot a confused look at his father, then to Wyatt, who shook his head. Watching them leave, he decided this was his chance to question Jasper about him ordering Virgil to stop seeing Lily. Before he could shift to face his father, Monica entered the office, closing the door behind her.

Staring in disbelief, Virgil shot up, heading to the door. Monica stepped in front of him, blocking his exit.

"It's time we talked. All three of us, Virgil." Her soft, insistent voice stopped him from lifting her up and setting her aside.

"Why? There's no changing the past."

She looked at Jasper, who nodded. "True. It's past time you heard the truth."

His head whipped between his mother and father. He was tired of feeling played. "All right. But if I suspect you're not giving me the entire truth, I'll leave."

"Fair enough." Stepping around him, she took a seat next to Jasper. "Please, sit down, Virgil."

"I'll stand."

"He's as stubborn as you, Jasper."

"Always has been." Reaching out, his father took Monica's hand in his, a gesture which confused Virgil even more.

Running out of patience, he glared at them. "Let's get this over with. I still have work to do."

"Do you remember your Uncle Warren?" Jasper asked, sure Virgil would.

"He was your twin brother. I was ten when he died. What does he have to do with anything?"

"A great deal, I'm afraid. Do you recall we moved to Brilliance because he lived here?"

"He worked at the ranch."

"Right." Jasper picked up a cup, swallowing the now cold coffee. "Not long after you were born, Warren dated a woman in Brilliance. It didn't last long, as she was seeing someone else. When Warren found out, he ended their relationship."

"Okay." Virgil wanted his father to get on with it.

"The woman married within weeks of her breakup with Warren. About nine months later, she had a baby girl."

This had Virgil sitting straighter, a sense of foreboding wrapping around him.

"Warren confronted the woman, insisting she tell him if the baby was his. She insisted the girl belonged to her husband. Warren had no recourse, and put it behind him."

Monica leaned forward. "Back then, DNA tests weren't as available. Today, it would be much easier to determine paternity. Warren and I spoke quite a bit back then."

"Before you left us?" Bitterness laced his words.

Her eyes widened for a second before her expression closed. "Yes, before I left. Warren always believed the baby was his. When he died, he still believed the girl was his."

"He could've been right," Jasper added. "The girl has Warren's eyes and smile."

"And yours." As twins, Virgil knew she'd have characteristics of both brothers. Then a sick feeling had him almost doubling over. "Lily." He inhaled a deep breath, exhaling before breathing in another. Calming his breathing, his anxious gaze locked on Jasper. "Lily is Warren's daughter?"

"We don't know for sure, Virgil. A test was never done. Monica and I talked a couple times a year at the time you and Lily were a couple. She's the one who reminded me of the possibility Lily was Warren's."

"Which would make her my cousin?" Gritting his teeth, he paced to the window. "That's why you ordered me to stop seeing her."

Jasper's head bobbed in resignation. "Yes. I couldn't allow the relationship to continue given what I knew.

Warren was dead by then, and you and Lily were young. I thought the two of you would move on, meet someone else. I was so wrong."

Scrubbing a hand over his face, Virgil tried to come to terms with the possibility Lily and he could be related. "No."

Monica lifted a brow. "No?"

"She's not my cousin. I would've felt it in here." He tapped a fist over his heart.

"In that case, it's a simple matter to have a lab do a paternity test. Since Warren and Jasper are identical twins, a test can be done using your father's DNA."

"And Lily's," Virgil added.

Monica nodded. "Which means you'll have to tell her."

"And if she's a match with Jasper?" Virgil already knew the answer. His plans of marriage and children would go up in flames.

Standing, Monica walked to him, taking his hands in hers, surprised when he didn't jerk them away. "At least you'll know the truth."

Chapter Sixteen

Virgil slipped the phone away, a painful knot building in his gut. "She'll be home in an hour. I'm going to meet her there."

"Do you want your father or me to go with you?"

He looked at his mother, feeling disconnected, as if he were someone else watching this play out. "No. This is something I have to do on my own." Walking to Anson's liquor cabinet, he pulled out a bottle of scotch, stared at it, then put it back. "Nothing is going to help."

"There's a good chance Lily isn't Warren's daughter. A very good chance." Jasper shoved himself up. "This should've been done soon after her birth."

"From what you've said, her mother would've refused." Pressing palms against his eyes, Virgil let out an almost animalistic groan. "There's no longer a choice. We have to know the truth."

Walking to the door, his grim expression almost brought Monica to her knees. "Call if we can help in any way."

Nodding, he left the house. Climbing into his truck, he prayed to find the right words. He and Lily had a connection he couldn't imagine with another woman. There had been times in the past when they could finish each other's sentences. Given time, and her forgiveness, he believed marriage and children were in their future.

Gripping the steering wheel tight enough for his knuckles to turn white, he thought back to Jasper forbidding him from seeing her again. Why hadn't he been truthful back then? This could've been settled years ago. Any number of doctors could've ordered a DNA test, finding an answer within a few weeks. So much pain could've been avoided if Jasper had offered the truth.

Virgil thought about how he'd react if the tests came back showing a match. Everything would change. Lily would accept one of the job offers and move away, of that, he was certain. He'd stay on the ranch, build his dream home. Though it wouldn't be for Lily. The odds were good it would be for him alone.

Parking in front of her apartment, he stared straight ahead. Never had he envisioned his parents' explanation. Who could make up such a fantastic story? Closing his eyes, he pictured him and Lily talking, watching a movie, waking up next to each other on her much too short sofa.

A soft rapping on the passenger window drew him back to the reason he'd driven to town. She was so achingly beautiful with her honey-blonde hair, emerald green eyes, and olive complexion. The smile she offered cut him right through the heart.

The girl he fell in love with as a youth still owned his heart years later. In truth, Lily owned every part of him.

Climbing out, he walked around the truck. Before he allowed himself to think, he wrapped an arm around her waist, tugging her against him. Lowering his head, he captured her mouth with his. Expecting her to pull away, he groaned when her arms locked behind his neck. A horn honking forced them apart.

"What a nice hello." She latched onto his hand, walking with him to the front door, not noticing the trepidation etched on his face.

Tossing her purse on a chair, she went straight to her bedroom. "I'll be out in a minute. Feel free to get something to drink."

Staring after her, he shoved both hands into pockets. He wasn't thirsty, or hungry, or anything other than wishing he didn't have to deliver news which might ruin whatever relationship blossomed between them.

He knew kissing Lily or falling asleep in front of the television meant little. People kissed all the time without a relationship developing. Neither was a commitment to love or a future together, although he wanted both from Lily.

"Are you all right, Virgil? You don't look well."

He hadn't heard the bedroom door open, or sensed her approach. "I...we need to talk."

Shoulders slumping, the concern on her face morphed to resignation. Scooting past him, she headed to the kitchen. "This feels like déjà vu."

"It's not. What I have to say is important. You'll need to decide what to do about it."

Brows scrunching, she opened the refrigerator. "Water, lemonade, beer, wine, or I can make coffee or tea."

"Water is fine."

Grabbing two bottles, she handed one to him. "Shall we sit down?"

"Sure."

Lowering herself near the middle of the sofa, she studied him as he came toward her on leaden feet, not meeting her gaze. Waiting until he sat down, she moved closer.

"You're worrying me, Virgil."

"I'm worried too."

"So start talking."

Taking several gulps of water, he set the bottle aside. "I spoke to my parents."

"Jasper *and* Monica?"

He snorted. "Not my choice. Turned out to be for the best. Did your mother ever mention a man named Warren?"

"Warren?" She picked at the label on the bottle, considering the name. "I don't think so."

Mouth drawing into a tight line, he reached out to take her hand. "This is going to be hard to hear, but you must listen to all I have to say."

"I'm already not liking the direction this is going."

"I understand." He let out a shaky breath, then began. "Before your mother married your father…"

Several minutes later, Lily jumped up, and ran to her ensuite bath. Following, Virgil knelt down, holding long, golden hair off her face as she emptied her stomach into the toilet. When finished, he soaked a washcloth in warm water before handing it to her.

Rolling from her knees, she leaned against a wall, her face pale, eyes rimmed in red. After a moment, a bitter chuckle burst from her lips.

"As reasons for breaking up go, this one is a doozy." She tried to smile, not quite achieving her goal. "It's so bizarre, it must be the truth."

Sitting on the tile floor next to her, he took her hand in his. "There's a good chance your father is who you've always believed him to be. Monica and Jasper were being hyper-cautious."

"As they should've been. I just wish Jasper had been honest with you about the reason. We might've had this all sorted out years ago." Leaning her head against the wall, she closed her eyes. "Several reasons for Jasper's ultimatum occurred to me. None as bizarre as reality. So what happens next?"

"You'd know more about this than me. My understanding is there are two types of DNA tests. At home, which isn't admissible for legal purposes, or we go to a lab, which can be used legally."

"The at home tests would be faster. Having them done at a lab would include a technician to assist us interpret the results."

Virgil tucked a stray strand of hair behind her ear. "What's your preference?"

"The lab. Will Jasper agree to them doing the tests?"

"Whatever you decide is what he'll do."

Standing, he held out his hand, helping her up. The instant she stood, Lily stepped to the sink, brushing her teeth.

She motioned at the toilet. "I'm sorry about all this."

"Lily. I gave you plenty of reasons to lose your lunch. Don't worry about it. I'll get your water from the living room."

"I'll go with you. Do you think Jasper would be available tomorrow?"

"One way to find out." Making the call, he spoke with Jasper a few seconds before hanging up. "He's going with Anson to a horse auction tomorrow and the following day. He'll get the test done as soon as he returns."

"Good. I'll get mine done early tomorrow so it's ready when Jasper takes his test. It'll give me a chance to talk to my friend about our reason for the tests. He's very good, and discreet."

"He?"

"Thomas moved here about two years ago. We meet for coffee every few months. I don't know much about him except he wanted to get away from Seattle. He's dating someone from the radiology department."

The last was what he hoped to hear. A chance existed that after the test results, Lily and he would be cousins, ending his hope for a future with her. He prayed there wouldn't be a match.

"Let's find some place for dinner. Whatever you want." He headed to the door without waiting for a response.

"Wait." Joining him at the door, she laid a hand on his arm. "Promise me something."

"Anything."

"I'm so tired of feeling hurt and angry over the breakup. If the tests show a match, promise me we'll still be friends."

Cupping her face with both hands, he brushed a kiss across her lips, sadness claiming him. "I'll promise to try, though it may take time. Would you accept one of the jobs and leave?"

Knowing the reason for the breakup lessened much of the pain. Trust was still an issue. If the results matched, she knew the biggest obstacle to staying in Brilliance would be watching Virgil date other women. At some point, he'd fall in love, marry, and have children. Lily knew she couldn't remain and watch.

"If the tests show a relationship, yes, I'll leave Brilliance."

"And if there isn't a match?"

"I don't know."

Jasper ate the simple dinner of beef stew, his mind on the upcoming test. Across the table, Monica watched him, knowing he had a great deal on his mind.

"Are you looking forward to the horse auction?" She'd been to many over her years with Jasper and afterward.

"Not as much as when I was younger. Anson's determined to find a few older mares and geldings perfect for trail rides. I don't know why he's bothering. Virgil has a small herd of twenty, which are fine for the new venture."

"Anson wants to be involved. The doctor and Margie are all over him about his diet, rest, sleep, and stress. Before you ask, no, I don't blame her at all. It's good she's a strong woman, and the doctor backs her up. Without her, Anson would've back pedaled by now, filling up on junk, smoking cigars, and all manner of nonsense. The same as you, he's had a lot of changes in his life. He needs something important to latch onto, a way to contribute to the dude ranch. Few men are as good at evaluating horses than you and Anson. This is a good thing for both of you."

"Maybe. This isn't the best time to be away." He chewed a small bite of stew before pushing the plate away.

"Don't like my cooking?"

"Your cooking's fine. My appetite is fading."

Setting down her fork, she waited until he looked at her. "The test will be what it will be, Jasper. I know you want it to show no relationship. I want the same. No use worrying about something you can't change."

"Knowing and accepting are two different things."

She remained silent when he stood, filling his cup with coffee before taking a look outside at the darkening sky. "There's something else. We need to be honest with Virgil about why you left."

Her chair scraped across the wood plank floor. Standing, she closed the short distance between them.

"Are you sure that's what you want?"

"Not sure at all. But it's past time. I should've explained years ago. Instead, I let him build his own conclusions. The boy needs to know."

"If you believe it's for the best. All I ask is we do this after the DNA tests."

Looking down at her, Jasper settled an arm over her shoulders. "You'll be there?"

"Yes."

Breathing out a relieved sigh, he lowered his head, covering her mouth with his.

Chapter Seventeen

Lily woke from a deep sleep, not ready to leave the comfort of her bed. The last couple days had been agonizingly slow. She'd completed her blood test at the lab. Jasper would be going in today, allowing the lab to determine if a connection existed. She expected the results within days.

She groaned at the sound of her phone. Reaching toward the bedside table, she looked at the screen. Virgil. Even with the unknowns, she couldn't help a small thrill.

"Hello."

"Good morning, beautiful."

"Hello, handsome." The exchange had been their traditional greeting when in high school.

Virgil had called each morning and evening since telling her what he'd learned from Jasper and Monica. They spent a scant fifteen minutes talking before work, stretching this to almost two hours each evening.

Lily knew falling for Virgil a second time was a big risk. If the tests showed a match, they'd be cousins, and anything more than basic affection would be forbidden. She'd been truthful when admitting to leaving Brilliance if their DNA matched.

"You're off today, right?"

She'd shared her schedule with Virgil the night before. "I am. And tomorrow."

"Come out to the ranch. We can take a trail ride. I might be able to talk Wyatt and Daisy into joining us."

Throwing off her covers, she snatched jeans, a shirt, and boots from her closet. "Can I ride Jiminy?"

She could hear the smile in his answer. "He's your horse. You can ride him whenever you want."

"I've never accepted him as a gift."

"Maybe not in words. Jiminy was meant for you, Lily. Come out and ride with us."

"I'd love to come out. I'll be there soon." Ending the call, she rushed through her morning ritual, getting dressed in record time. Grabbing her hat, gloves, and a jacket, she hurried outside.

Lily parked by the barn less than twenty minutes later. Waiting nearby, Virgil helped her out, pulling her into his arms for a deep kiss. Her hands pushing on his chest had him pulling away.

He looked down into green eyes etched with worry. "What is it?"

"Maybe we shouldn't be doing this until we get the test results. What if..." Lily let her voice fade, unable to finish.

"I know you're right. It isn't smart. From now on, no more kissing. Holding hands is fine though, right?" His wide grin had her laughing.

"Fine. But nothing more. Do I need to tack up Jiminy?"

"Already done. Did you have time to eat?"

She shook her head. "I was in too big a hurry to get out here."

"Anxious to see me?" When Virgil studied her face, he saw a flash of sadness. Cupping her face in his hands, he stared into her eyes. "No sadness today, sweetheart. We'll deal with the results when we have them." Placing a lingering kiss on her forehead, he reluctantly dropped his hands. "Let's rustle you up some food. Nacho made several breakfast casseroles this morning."

"I love those."

Taking her hand, he started toward the kitchen door. "I know."

Standing aside for Lily to enter first, he spotted Emma at the stove while Nacho worked with the leftovers. "Lily hasn't eaten yet. What do you have?"

"Four helpings of the casserole and some potatoes. The bacon and sausage are long gone. Of course, you know that, Virgil. You ate half of each."

"Hey! I fought Wyatt for every bite. Dish Lily up casserole and whatever potatoes you have left. I'll get her orange juice."

Nacho shot her a smile. "Coming right up."

She'd noticed how Nacho's attitude had improved since the Bonners had hired Emma. Even saying the woman's name had his stomach clenching. If the DNA found she and the Redstars were related, would Virgil turn his attention to Emma?

"Good morning, Lily."

She turned to see Emma holding out a heaping plate of food to her. "Oh, thank you. This looks delicious."

"The ranch hands always inhale the casserole whenever Nacho makes it. I'm surprised there was any left." Reaching into a pocket of her apron, Emma handed her utensils. "Are you going riding?"

"We are. I think Wyatt and Daisy will be joining us." She set her plate down on a counter in front of a large window offering a view to the west. Virgil joined her, placing a glass of fresh orange juice by her plate. "This casserole is so good."

"No one makes it better than Nacho. I hope he passes the recipe to Emma when he retires."

Taking a sip of juice, she looked between the two cooks. "Has he given notice?"

"Not yet, but Wyatt expects it within a year. He wants to be certain Emma is ready to take over. She'll hire her own replacement." He placed a hand on the small of her back. "Wyatt and Daisy will meet us by the horses in fifteen minutes."

Scooping up the last bite of casserole onto the fork, she held it up for Virgil. He didn't hesitate to accept her offering.

"We have to talk about Jiminy."

"What do we need to talk about?"

"Well, for one, what if the results don't show what we want?"

His features sobered. "If you're asking if I'll expect you to give him back, you're wrong. Jiminy is yours, Lily."

"What if I take another job?"

"You can leave him here, or stable him closer to where you work. I'll be the one to deliver him to new stables, though. So select carefully."

The glow in her eyes dimmed. "I hate this waiting."

"I know, sweetheart. So do I." Running a hand over her hair, he squeezed her shoulder. "It will work out."

Heart pounding, she nodded. "I hope you're right."

"I'm so glad you made it out, Lily. There's something I want to talk to you about." Daisy rode next to her, both behind the men.

"Uh-oh. Whenever you say those words, I end up working on one of your projects."

"This is a good one, Lily. I promise you'll have a great time."

"You do remember we're already working on next year's calendar."

Daisy waved her hand in the air. "This one's easy. One afternoon of prep, and one day on-site."

"All right, enough buttering me up. Give me details."

"You know the Spring Fling Festival is this weekend, right?"

"I do."

"The Battered Women's Center doesn't have enough volunteers to man the cake booth. They don't have enough food, either. The director asked if I could help. I'm asking if you can take a shift."

"And?"

"You know me too well. And do you have time to donate five cakes and five batches of cupcakes?" She had the good sense to wince at the amounts.

"Five cakes? Wow. That's a lot of baking, Daiz."

"I know. If you have a day off, we could bake together. The ranch would be best since we have a couple large ovens."

"I have plenty of time. When I decided to consider other options, I talked to human resources. Somehow, I've accumulated six weeks of vacation. I'm taking the next two weeks off."

The women followed the men onto a trail heading southwest. Lily wondered if Virgil wanted to check the eagle's nest. She hoped so.

"Come out to the ranch and bring clothes to spend the night. We can bake for two days and get everything done. Maybe bake more than five cakes each."

"Or more cupcakes. People love them. They'll buy a dozen at a time. Do you have recipes of what you want to make?"

"The center's director sent over favorites from past events. A total of six. They can be converted to cupcakes. Nacho gave me a couple cake recipes, and Lydia at the bakery gave me four of her best."

"Count me in."

"Wonderful. Okay. Now, tell me what's going on with you and Virgil."

Lily looked ahead at Virgil's back, wondering if he'd shared anything with Wyatt. If so, then Daisy would already know some of it.

"I've been offered jobs at the two hospitals I visited. Both are excellent opportunities."

Daisy gave her a disbelieving look. "Can we not talk about you leaving town? I'll be miserable the rest of the day."

Ever since learning the truth about their breakup, Lily had a hard time seeing herself somewhere besides Brilliance. So much depended on the outcome of the tests.

"You're right. I haven't made up my mind. It's not that leaving is what I want."

"I know, Lil. Your future seems tied to Virgil."

"After all this time. How can I still have feelings for him eight years later?"

"Because he's the love of your life. The same as Wyatt is the love of mine. Moving on is almost impossible when you've experienced such a soul deep passion. Is there a chance you and Virgil could have a future?"

"There's always a chance, right?" Lily prayed she and Virgil might still have a future.

"That's my belief. Do you remember how Anson tried hard to keep Wyatt and me apart?"

"He had his reasons, even if they were wrong."

Daisy smiled. "Anson and I get along very well now. He treats me as a daughter instead of an interloper. If I'd given up, Wyatt and I wouldn't be married."

Lily knew how hard Daisy worked to win Anson's approval. She was proud of her friend for sticking it out.

"I heard about the tests."

The comment surprised Lily. "Virgil told Wyatt?"

"He told both of us. The burden of hurting you has weighed on him for years. The pain he caused stayed with him every day. Knowing the reason lifted a tremendous amount of guilt off his shoulders. Have you forgiven him?"

"Yes. I'm learning how to trust him again." Lily looked away before returning her gaze to Daisy. "If the tests show I'm related to Jasper..."

"They won't. I'm certain of it."

"How do you know?"

Daisy placed a hand over her heart. "Because you and Virgil deserve a chance at a future together."

Lily prayed her friend was right.

Chapter Eighteen

"Are you still accepting cakes?" Lydia, owner of Brilliance Coffee & Bakery, set a large box on the table. A chocolate mousse cake and carrot cake, both decorated on the top and sides, were inside.

"We sure are. Someone is going to be real lucky to get one." Lily lifted one out while Lydia held the box steady.

"There's another in the car. I'll be right back."

Placing the cakes inside a large cabinet with glass front, Lily took a step back to view the offerings. It had been a lot of work over five days to find volunteers to bake cakes and cupcakes. The time had been worth every minute.

"Did I just see Lydia?" Daisy joined Lily, a box holding two dozen cupcakes in her hands.

"She brought two cakes and is retrieving a third from her car. I'm so glad you were able to find the cabinet. It's perfect for displaying baked goods."

"The mayor mentioned a storage unit where the town keeps items left behind when businesses close. He had no issue with us using it. I may offer to buy the cabinet for my shop."

"We could use it year after year," Lily added. "New paint might help it fit in with your shop."

"I thought the same."

Lily watched as other vendors set up their booths. "Do you have a minute to help me with the banner?"

"I'll do that."

The women turned to Virgil standing a few feet away. "No offense, but you two could use some height."

Daisy stuck out her tongue, smiling as she did it. "We never turn down help. Did Wyatt come to town with you?"

"He's right behind me. Stopped to help Doc Worrel hang her banner." Virgil mentioned the veterinarian. "Dorie hired a vet technician a few weeks ago. He'll be here about the time the public arrives." Tall and tan with glorious red hair, the woman was kind, with a huge heart. At one time, Daisy thought Wyatt held an interest in the stunning doctor.

Jogging toward them, Wyatt wrapped arms around Daisy, giving his wife a kiss. "How are you ladies doing?"

"They need help hanging their banner. You take one end and I'll take the other." Virgil picked up one corner, testing the swivel claw hook. Wyatt did the same on the other corner before lifting it into place.

Daisy and Lily stood back, watching as the men secured the banner identifying the booth as benefiting the women's center. They gave them a thumbs up.

"Looks great. Thanks." Daisy turned to talk to a friend, another downtown business owner while Lily stepped behind the table. Loaded with cupcakes, she kept them covered with a clear, plastic top.

Virgil strode up beside her, his gaze moving over the table. "You should have a successful day."

"Hope so. I'd love to sell all the donated food."

An awkward silence fell between them. They'd spoken twice since the ride at the ranch, each time avoiding the topic which could change their lives.

"Jasper called the lab yesterday. They still haven't determined if there's a match." Virgil placed a hand on her shoulder. "I'm not worried."

"At least one of us isn't."

"Whatever the results, we'll still be friends, Lily. I wish my father had explained when he'd first warned me away from you. This could've been settled years ago."

"Nothing we can do about it now except wait for the results." She reached out, threading her fingers through his.

"Do you know what you'll do if a match exists?" He squeezed her hand.

"Leave. You know I won't be able to stay. It would be too hard on us to watch the other marry and have a family. Leaving will mean each of us has the opportunity for a fresh start."

"I'm not interested in a fresh start with anyone but you, Lily."

Since learning she may be Virgil's blood relation, she'd done a great deal of thinking. They could never get the years back. She saw no sense in dwelling on what could've been if Jasper had explained himself.

A family walked up. Their clothes were clean, yet threadbare in some places. The boy's pants an inch shorter than they should be.

The boy pointed at the cupcakes. "Can I have one, Mommy?"

Letting go of Virgil's hand, relief washed over Lily for the interruption. She didn't want to spend another minute dwelling on the possible results or what ifs.

The husband pulled out his wallet. "How much are they?"

"Fifty cents."

He glanced at his wife, son, and daughter. "Does everyone want one?"

"I do. I do." The boy jumped up and down.

The woman lowered her voice, touching her husband's arm. "Can we afford them?"

Hearing the question, Lily spoke up. "I don't have the sign made yet, but we're selling four for a dollar and fifty cents."

"Then we'll have four. Go ahead, kids. Pick which one you want, but let the lady hand them to you." He laughed when his children lit up as if it were Christmas. When they were finished, he looked at his wife. "Honey?"

"Are those coconut cupcakes?"

"They are. Lydia, at the bakery, made them."

"I'd like one, please." She watched as her son and daughter took large bites of theirs.

Lily handed the largest one to her, along with a napkin, before looking at the husband. "And what would you like?"

"The carrot cake looks awfully good."

"They are," Virgil spoke up, grinning. "Daisy Bonner made them. I bought one earlier."

The man straightened at the name. "Bonner?"

"They own Whistle Rock Ranch."

"Do you know if they're hiring?" The hope in the man's voice tore at Lily.

"We might be. Do you have experience on a ranch?"

"I've worked with cattle and horses all my life. I also work on farm equipment."

"Dad can fix anything," the boy said, his mouth full of cupcake.

Virgil couldn't help a grin at the boy's declaration. "Is that so?"

Nodding vigorously, he took another bite of the chocolate confection.

Reaching into his pocket, Virgil pulled out a card. "We're always looking for experienced men. Directions to the ranch are on the back. Come by anytime Monday and ask for me."

Grabbing it, he stuck out his hand. "I'll be there Monday."

Virgil accepted the outstretched hand. "I'm Virgil Redstar."

"Owen Baker. Thank you."

"Bring references, Mr. Baker."

"I sure will."

"Bye." The young boy waved as he followed his parents.

"That was good of you, Virgil."

"As I told him, we're always looking for good men. No matter his experience, I'll need to check his references." He continued to watch the man while Lily spoke to a couple debating over buying a dozen cupcakes or a regular cake.

Boxing their selection, she handed them change. "Thanks so much. It's for a good cause."

Within seconds, another couple and a lone woman walked up. The pace didn't slacken, Lily and Virgil selling the baked goods until there were only a few cakes and three dozen cupcakes left.

"This is fabulous. I sure hope the team tomorrow is bringing a bunch of cakes. It's a group of teachers who are volunteering. I'm pretty sure they'll get their colleagues and maybe some parents to contribute. If we hit six hundred dollars, there's an anonymous donor who's going to match it."

"Doubt that's going to be a problem, Lily. You're already at almost five hundred for today."

"Really?" She'd saw Virgil counting the money, never dreaming it had grown so much.

"You started with fifty dollars in change. There's five hundred forty in the box. You still have three more hours today, plus tomorrow."

Bouncing on the balls of her feet, she reminded Virgil of the little boy from that morning. "That's amazing. I can't wait to tell Daisy."

Watching her reaction, his heart danced in his chest. He knew there'd never be another woman for him. Lily was it. She always had been.

"Virgil! Is that you?" An attractive woman with mahogany hair and a bright smile walked straight toward him.

Recognition hit him. "Mel?"

"It's me." She reached up on her toes to kiss his cheek. "It's been, what? Three years." Taking a step back, she looked him up and down. "If possible, I do believe you look even better than in college." She glanced at Lily. "He was always a catch."

"Uh, Melissa. This is my close friend, Lily Cardoza. Lily, Melissa Conrad. We knew each other in college."

Melissa stuck out her hand. "Call me Mel."

Lily shook her hand, face a mask as she took in the beautiful woman. "Nice meeting you."

"Same here. So, Virgil. Is this where you live?"

He shot a look at Lily, knowing the timing couldn't be worse for Melissa showing up. They had gone out a few times over a couple months before deciding they were better friends than anything more.

"A little north of here at Whistle Rock Ranch."

"No way." She whirled around, motioning for another woman to join her. "Jill. Get over here." Returning her attention to Virgil, Melissa took another glance at Lily. "Have you known Virgil long?"

"Since I was ten."

"What's so important you pulled me away from the hunky cowboy over there?"

"Jill, this is Virgil Redstar. We dated in college. Virgil, this is Jill Ames, my best friend since kindergarten."

He shook the hand Jill extended. "Ma'am."

"You aren't going to believe this. Virgil works at the dude ranch we signed up for. Isn't that amazing?"

Jill's gaze wandered over him before a slow smile curved her lips. "Well then, it's very good to meet you, Virgil." Flipping long, brown hair over a shoulder, she looked at Lily. "I'm Jill."

"Lily."

Heading off the collision he saw coming, Virgil settled an arm over Lily's shoulders, tucking her close. "Lily is a nurse at the local hospital."

"How nice." Jill gave her a cursory glance before latching back onto Virgil. "So what do you do at the ranch?"

Not used to being dismissed, Lily stepped in front of Virgil, feeling his arms come around her waist. "He's the foreman, horse trainer extraordinaire, and my significant other."

Chapter Nineteen

Virgil was still laughing later that evening while he and Lily prepared dinner at her apartment. "Significant other?"

She pointed the knife used to slice vegetables at him. "One of us had to step up. Those women were looking at you all wrong."

Again, he laughed. "All wrong, huh?"

Focusing on the squash she cut into cubes, she stopped, spearing him with a skeptical look. "You can't tell me you didn't feel their eyes on you. Especially Jill's." She turned back to the cutting board on the counter.

Stepping behind her, he wrapped his arms around her waist, tugging her against his chest. "Jill isn't my type."

"What about Melissa? You dated her in college."

"We went out four or five times. Nothing serious." He fought the urge to kiss her neck.

"But she's more your type." Grabbing a zucchini, she sliced it into quarter inch thick discs.

"She's a city girl who enrolled at the U of W to meet cowboys. There were a lot of men who took her out. As I recall, she transferred to the University of Colorado her junior year. Today was the first time I've seen her in years."

"I should sign up for the same week at the dude ranch."

"Why is that?"

"To protect you from women like Melissa and Jill. They're vipers."

Head tilting back, he roared with laughter. "Tell you what. You can go on the trail ride the week they're at the ranch. Unless they take lessons, the trail rides are the only times I'll be around them." Resting his head on the top of her head, he breathed in the clean scent of her hair.

"Are you sure?"

"Of course. You're welcome on any of the trail rides." Although this discussion would be meaningless if the DNA tests came back showing a match.

Setting the knife down, she leaned against him. "This waiting is difficult."

"I know, sweetheart."

"After being apart for so long, I can't stand the thought of not seeing you again." The quiver in her voice knocked the wind from him.

"Don't think that way." Turning her to face him, he took a small step back. "How about we talk about anything except the tests?"

"I'd like that." Ignoring their earlier agreement, she rested her hands on his shoulders, going on her toes to kiss his chin. "So, what do you want to talk about?" Turning back to the counter, she continued cutting vegetables.

He leaned against the counter a few inches from her, crossing his arms. "I have some good news. More than good."

"Yeah? Tell me."

"Did Daisy tell you she and Wyatt are going to start building their house west of the ranch?"

"She mentioned Anson had deeded them land for a place of their own. Have they already drawn up plans?"

"They're working on them now. With the regular ranch work and dude ranch, I doubt they'll get much done before the snow falls."

"Is their house what you wanted to tell me?" She swept the vegetables into an already heated skillet, sprinkling them with seasoning. Opening the oven door, she checked the rest of their dinner.

"No. The Bonner family decided to deed me two hundred acres next to Wyatt's property."

Eyes wide, she tossed the hot pads on the counter as a broad smile curved the corners of her mouth. "That's fabulous news."

"The documents were signed a little more than a week ago and recorded. The land is mine, Lily."

Wrapping her arms around his neck, she hugged him tight. "I'm so happy for you." Dropping her arms, she moved back to the counter. Her smile remained.

"I offered to pay. Wyatt and Anson refused."

"I'm not surprised. You're another brother to Wyatt and a fourth son to Anson and Margie. They see you as family."

157

When the timer buzzed, she removed pork chops and potatoes from the oven. Filling plates, she set one in front of Virgil, then brought hers to the table. Picking up her fork, she leaned toward him.

"Tell me all about your plans for the property."

Lily took a break from her morning shift at the hospital, going outside to make a call to Sheridan. She hadn't heard back from the human resources person since leaving a message over a week earlier.

Leaving another message, she slid the phone back into her pocket. She'd return it to her locker at the end of her break. Opening the door to go back inside, her phone buzzed. The Sheridan hospital's number appeared.

"Hello?"

"Ms. Cardoza?"

"Yes, this is Lily Cardoza."

"I'm so sorry about the delay getting back to you. There was a terrible accident a week ago. One of our doctors was seriously injured in what we believe was a hit-and-run. It's been hard on everyone."

"I'm so sorry. I hope the doctor is recovering."

"I'm afraid recovering is going to be very slow. Anyway, the committee reviewing hiring recommendations postponed their meeting until next week. I'm sorry for the delay, and understand if you need to move on to another offer."

"I completely understand, and there's no rush. There is one other offer which interests me at a hospital in southern Wyoming."

"Opposite sides of the state," the woman said.

Chuckling, Lily nodded, even though the woman couldn't see her. "Yes. Would it be all right to call you later this week?"

"Of course. I may have more news for you. Thank you for your understanding."

"I do hope the doctor recovers soon."

"We all do, Ms. Cardoza."

Ending the call, Lily checked the time. She still had five minutes. Doing an internet search concerning a hit-and-run in Sheridan, several articles appeared. Selecting one, she scanned the article and gasped.

"No."

Stumbling to a nearby bench, she read through the account of the accident, then lowered the phone to her lap. "I can't believe it."

The victim was Doctor Mason Nagle, the emergency room doctor who'd given her the tour of the hospital. The man who'd made her laugh at dinner the same night. A Rockies baseball fan, the same as Lily.

The article didn't go into detail on his injuries, although she knew his condition must've been grave. Might still be grave judging by the deep concern in the voice of the woman in human resources. Lowering her head, she sent up a quick prayer for his full recovery.

Walking back inside, the image of Mason drinking beer and laughing stayed branded on her mind during the rest of her shift. The drive home didn't include the usual music or thoughts of Virgil.

Tossing her purse on the sofa, she headed to her computer. Over the next hour, she read every article the search pulled up. As most bits of news, there was a rash of information the first day or so, then nothing more. Follow-up was rare, even for a much respected doctor. Closing the screen, a thought hit her.

Locating the name of the steakhouse in Sheridan, she dialed the number. "Is Harry working tonight?"

"Hold on."

A moment later, the bartender picked up the phone. "It's Harry."

"I doubt you'll remember me, but Mason Nagle and I had dinner at the bar a couple weeks ago."

"Lily, right?"

"Good memory. I wondered if you had any information on his recovery."

"The hit-and-run driver did a real number on him. I've been to the hospital a couple times, but was only allowed in his room for five minutes once. Looked like he'd been run over by a big rig."

"Did they tell you anything about his injuries or current condition?"

"I'm surprised they let me see him at all. Usually, it's relatives only. His parents were there and gave their approval for me to poke my head into his room. They told me he has two broken legs, a broken arm, fractured ribs, a concussion, and some internal injuries, which required surgery. My understanding is they didn't expect him to make it through the night. The guy's got a massive will to live. He improves some each day. His father went home, but his mother is still in town. I have her phone number if you want it."

"Thanks, Harry, but it's one thing for them to give it to you. Another for you to pass it along to someone else."

"Yeah, you're right."

"Any idea when he'll be released?"

"None. Give me your number and I'll call when I learn anything else."

Lily rattled off her number. "Thanks. Is it okay if I check back with you?"

"Anytime, sweetheart. I'll tell the doctor you asked about him."

Ending the call, she leaned back in the chair, covering her face with both hands. She still couldn't wrap her head around the fact the vibrant, quick-witted, and brutally handsome doctor might never be the same.

She jumped when her phone chimed. Not wanting to speak with anyone right then, she let it go to voicemail. Heading to the kitchen, she grabbed a bottle of beer. Removing the top, she held the bottle in the air.

"To Doctor Mason Nagle. Here's to your full recovery."

Swallowing a few sips, she set the beer down. As she did, her phone chimed again.

Letting out a breath, she hesitated before walking back to the dining room, where it sat next to her computer. Seeing the name, she grabbed it.

"Hey. Do you have news for me?"

"I do. Hope it's what you want to hear."

For a moment, she considered telling her friend she'd call him back. Inhaling a deep breath, she exhaled slowly.

"Go ahead and tell me."

"There's no match between you and Jasper Redstar."

She gripped the phone tighter. "Say that again."

"There's no match, Lily. I hope this is what you wanted to hear."

She rushed her response. "Yes. Yes, it is. Thanks so much. I owe you."

Chapter Twenty

Lily sat on the edge of the sofa, the bottle of beer resting on the coffee table, the phone in her lap. It had been several minutes since she'd learned the results of the tests. She couldn't get her racing heart under control. At least her breathing had returned to normal.

She glanced at her phone. Two calls had to be made. The first to Virgil.

Lily hoped his previous declarations of love were true. She hated the pang of doubt, not being certain of his reaction. As much as her heart claimed him, her mind hadn't yet accepted he could be trusted.

Picking up the phone, she stared at it before setting it back down. Putting off the call wouldn't help. Taking a deep, fortifying breath, she chastised herself for being a coward.

She'd received good news, and had to believe Virgil would agree. They were now free to be together, or go their separate ways. What would he choose now that the results were known?

Grabbing the phone, she rose to her feet, pacing to the window. Calling Virgil, she braced herself for his reaction.

"Hey, Lily. Can you hold on for a minute?"

"Yeah. Sure." Her heart pounded an almost painful rhythm in her chest. Hard enough she thought it might explode.

"Sorry about that. We're vaccinating some of the horses. How are you?"

They hadn't seen each other since he left her apartment Saturday evening. She'd helped at the festival again on Sunday before going out to dinner with a group of volunteers.

"Good."

"Good, huh? What..." His voice trailed off. Then she could hear him clearing his voice.

"Virgil?"

"I'm here," he whispered. "Did you get the results?"

"Yes." Her heart continued to hammer.

"And?"

"There isn't a match." The silence on the other end of the phone stretched until she began pacing. She was just about to say his name when an ear-piercing yelp came through the phone.

"Virgil?"

"That's wonderful news, sweetheart. Let me finish up here and I'll drive to your place. I'll take you out to celebrate."

The tightness in her throat began to ease. "So you're happy with the results?"

"Of course I'm happy. Aren't you?"

"Very. Dinner would be perfect."

"All right. I'll see you as soon as I can get there. And, Lily?"

"Yes?"

"I love you."

Virgil hung up before she could respond.

Lily couldn't shake the unsettled feeling lodged in her chest. She didn't know if concerns about her and Virgil, the news about Dr. Nagle, or a combination of both had triggered her unease. Regardless of the source, she stood at a crossroad.

Virgil would expect her commitment to a second chance. She didn't blame him, yet she still wavered.

The last few weeks had opened her eyes to other possibilities. She'd learned the value of her education, skills, and experience. As one of the interviewers had explained, Lily was quite marketable. He'd suggested she understand her value and be selective when making a decision.

Knowing the results of the tests, did she want to uproot her life, leave friends behind, and accept an opportunity hours from Brilliance? The search had begun because of what she perceived as Virgil's lack of interest. She now knew her assumptions had been wrong.

A knock signaled Virgil had arrived. Opening the door, she let out a surprised laugh when he thrust a beautiful bouquet of pink and yellow roses toward her.

"Oh my. These are gorgeous."

"For a gorgeous woman." Stepping inside, he took her in his arms, lowering his mouth for a searing kiss. "Been wanting to do that for a while now." Kissing her again, he whirled her around until she giggled.

"Virgil. Put me down."

"I don't think I will." Deepening their kiss, he got lost in having her close. Several seconds ticked by before he set her on the floor.

Running a hand over her hair, she let out a shaky breath. "Well, that was definitely one fine kiss, Mr. Redstar."

"There'll be more, Ms. Cardoza."

"I'm counting on it." Holding up the roses, she pulled down a vase from a kitchen cupboard. "Could you hand me the pair of shears in the drawer beside you?"

He did, watching as she trimmed the stems before arranging them and adding water. "They're stunning, Virgil. Thank you."

Walking past him, she set the vase on the coffee table. "Did you say anything to Jasper about the results?"

"He knows. The results are bittersweet for him."

Crossing her arms, her brows knit together. "Why?"

"Jasper's happy we have a future. He feels bad about his decision taking years away from us."

"He did what he thought was right." Dropping her arms, she moved past him to the dining room, closing her laptop. "It may have been for the best. We might have married too soon, before we were ready."

Stepping closer, he tucked a strand of honey-blonde hair behind her ear. "I told him the same." Picking up a light jacket Lily had draped over a chair, he held it out. "Are you ready to get dinner? This is supposed to be a celebration."

Slipping into the jacket, she grabbed her purse from the sofa. "Where are we going?"

"I thought we'd walk to the new Mexican restaurant on the corner." Holding out his hand, she threaded her fingers through his.

Lifting his bottle of beer, Virgil held it up until Lily lifted hers. "Here's to us, and our shared future." Tapping the mouths of their bottles, each swallowed some of the local brew.

Their table looked out onto the street and a clear night punctuated with a full moon. Lily stared outside while Virgil placed their orders, her fingers peeling small pieces off the bottle's label.

Thrilled at the test results, her thoughts kept returning to Mason Nagle. Well respected and liked, her heart broke at what she guessed would be a long road to recovery.

"What are you thinking about?" Lifting the bottle, he drank a long swallow of beer.

Lily hadn't intended to tell Virgil about Mason, the dinner, or the hit-and-run. It didn't seem important. Before Wyatt married Daisy, she knew Virgil and Wyatt sometimes shared dinner with women when attending stock auctions out of town.

As a firm believer secrets always came back to bite you, she swallowed a small sip of beer.

"The emergency doctor who gave me a tour of the Sheridan hospital was involved in a hit-and-run after I drove home. He's alive, his prognosis is good, but healing will take quite a while. He's one of the docs I'll work with if I take the position." She winced, realizing what she'd said.

Virgil stilled at her comment, the bottle of beer partway to his mouth. The last words hit him in the gut with surprising intensity. "You're still thinking about leaving?"

Cocking her head, Lily could see the shock in his pinched features. "I haven't made up my mind."

"My understanding was you'd be staying if the tests showed no match. Was I wrong?"

"No. Yes. I don't know." Running fingers through her hair, she combed the golden strands away from her face. "Going to Sheridan and Laramie opened my mind to other opportunities. The hospital here doesn't offer the experiences I'd receive in other places."

Setting the beer down, he leaned against the back of the chair, crossing his arms. "I see."

She reached out to lay a hand on his arm, then pulled it back. His body language expressed the confusion and anger he fought to keep tucked inside.

Neither took their eyes off the other when the waitress set their meals in front of them. Nor did they pick up their forks to eat. Seconds turned to minutes as Virgil processed her startling admission. Lifting his hand, he signaled the waitress for another beer.

As their dinner grew cold, Lily shifted in her chair, sorting out what to say. Nothing she came up with would remove the tense pain from his face.

"Here you are." The woman's focus turned to Lily. "Another beer for you too?"

Lily shook her head. "Um, no. This is fine. Thank you."

Taking a long draw of beer, he set the bottle down while ignoring the heaping plate of food. Slowly rising, he reached into his pocket, tossing more than enough bills on the table to cover their meal and tip.

"Virgil?"

"I'm going to head back to the ranch. Are you all right walking home by yourself?"

"Yes, but—" His hand rose, stopping whatever else she intended to say.

"Let me know what you decide. I'd appreciating hearing it from you rather than Daisy or Wyatt."

"Don't leave. Sit down and we'll talk."

Staring at her, his jaw tight, he gave a sharp shake of his head. "It would be better for me to head back to the ranch. You've got decisions to make, and us talking isn't going to get that done."

When she started to shove her chair back to stand, he again held up his hand. "I'd rather walk back to the truck alone. I've got my own thinking to do."

Mouth open, heart hammering, she watched him stalk to the door, leaving her alone.

"Well, that didn't go so well." The whispered words did nothing to calm the ache building in her chest.

She'd made a complete mess of the evening. He'd offered a celebratory meal and she'd tossed it in his face.

"Was everything all right with your meals?" The waitress stared down at the still full plates.

"Yes. He, uh...had to leave. Would you mind boxing the meals?"

"Not at all, honey. I sure do know what it's like to be married to a man whose schedule isn't his own. You'll get used to it, though."

Lily didn't consider correcting the woman's assumption about her and Virgil being married. She could barely wrap her mind around how a few misspoken words had ruined their evening.

Lily hadn't made any firm decisions about taking one of the offered positions. Both offered challenges she might never face in Brilliance.

Is that what she wanted? Challenges in her work versus a future with Virgil? All these years, she'd waited for another chance. Had she blown it with a few careless words?

Her love for Virgil hadn't lessened at all since high school. The test results should've cleared up any remaining doubt about being with him. He hadn't broken up with her because he didn't love her. He'd done it at Jasper's insistence.

They'd both suffered over the years due to his father's concerns about parentage. If those concerns had never surfaced, she had no doubt they'd be married, perhaps with one or two children.

Deep down, did she truly believe she couldn't trust him?

"Here you go. All wrapped and ready for the fridge." The waitress looked down at the bills on the table. "Do you need change?"

"No. Thank you for boxing everything up."

"Hope you come back again. Trust me, the food is outrageous."

Even with the way the evening ended, Lily found herself smiling.

The walk to her apartment wasn't long at all. Three buildings, a left turn, and she found herself at the front door. She'd hoped Virgil would be waiting for her. The empty porch testified to the extent of his anger.

Let me know what you decide.

His parting words haunted her as she changed clothes, brushed her teeth, and slid under the covers. She knew sleep would be hard to find.

Lily found herself thinking about Daisy, and how much she'd miss her best friend if she moved away. She'd even miss her crazy ideas, which always seemed to work, the trail rides, and long talks. Marriage meant there were a few more miles between them. Not the hundred there'd be if Lily left town.

Staring at the ceiling, she thought of the two hundred acres and house Virgil intended to build. Would Lily be all right if another woman shared the home with him?

"Absolutely not." The two words echoed off the walls and ceiling. It didn't take a genius to realize what they said about her future.

Lily couldn't imagine one without Virgil in it.

Chapter Twenty-One

Virgil removed the last of the old horseshoes from a young mare in preparation for a new set. Their regular farrier had called earlier, apologizing for not being available. Seems his wife went into labor with their second child just as he was leaving the house.

Normally, Virgil would wait for him, but the mare had thrown a shoe three days earlier, and he didn't feel comfortable holding off any longer. He'd learned many farrier skills from the old man Anson had used for years. At least he seemed old to a twelve-year-old boy.

Virgil and Wyatt spent hours watching him, amazed at the man's easy rapport with even the most cantankerous horse. By the time he retired, forcing Anson to hire a replacement, both boys could do much of the farrier work without assistance.

"Doesn't appear you've forgotten anything." Wyatt walked into the area used by the farrier, watching as Virgil finished with the last shoe.

"Can't imagine doing this full time until I'm sixty." He referred to their original farrier. "We should've included massages as part of his pay." Setting down the last hoof, Virgil straightened, stretching his arms toward the ceiling.

"Daisy got a message from Lily. She'd like you to call her."

Virgil listened, not responding.

"Did you hear me?"

"Yeah."

"Are you going to call her?"

"Not really your business, Wyatt."

"Look. Lily is Daisy's best friend. If Lily is upset, so is Daisy, which means I'm not happy. Just give her a call, would you? I'll be meeting with the new hire."

"Owen Baker?"

"Yeah. The man you met at the festival. You do know he was recently released from the state prison in Laramie, right?"

Virgil set a tool aside, lifting another to clean it. "He told me when I interviewed him."

"Broke into a drug store to steal opioids."

Virgil turned toward Wyatt. "For his wife, who'd become addicted after back surgery. He didn't count on a silent alarm. It was his only offense. I'm surprised he didn't get off with time served and parole. Instead, he got a two year sentence. The owner of the drug store was a friend of the judge. He's the one who pushed for prison time."

Wyatt's mouth twisted into a grimace. "Wonder why? He must've known Owen had a wife and two children."

Virgil shot him a knowing gaze. "He didn't tell you?"

"What?"

"The drug store owner was his wife's father."

"Geez."

Virgil nodded. "Yeah. The man thought he could get his daughter to file for divorce. She refused. Took the kids and moved in with an aunt to wait out the sentence. Makes our fathers look like saints."

"You've got that right. Hope he works out. I'd better get up to the office." Wyatt started toward the house, then stopped. "And please call Lily."

Waving a hand in the air, Virgil returned to his work. He'd call Lily when he was darn well ready to, and not a second before.

Bracing his hands on the workbench, he dropped his head. He'd slept little since she'd stunned him at the restaurant, letting him know she might still accept a job away from Brilliance. Away from him.

Maybe walking out of the restaurant wasn't the best decision. He could've stayed, listened as she explained her reasons for leaving. After the good news about the tests, he'd never for a second considered she might still move. Sheridan or Laramie. Both too far away to see each other except on weekends.

Perhaps she thought a long-distance relationship would be good enough. Well, it wouldn't be near good enough for Virgil Redstar. And what about the doctor in

Sheridan? Something in her voice warned him she might've already developed feelings for the man.

Shoving away from the workbench, he ran a hand down his face, wishing he knew what to do. Leaving or staying was Lily's decision. He had no right to force his desires on her. If they'd been married, or engaged... But they weren't.

Leading the mare back to the stable, he forced a smile when spotting Wyatt approach with Owen. He had a good feeling about the new hire.

"Good to see you, Owen." Virgil held out his hand, giving a slight squeeze.

"I appreciate the opportunity."

"You'll be working with me and one of our best ranch hands, Barrel. We work with both the cattle and horses." Virgil continued with his usual speech, information he gave to all new hands. "I'll introduce you to Barrel. He'll get you started."

The phone in his pocket vibrated as he and Owen headed to the corral where Barrel and a few other men worked with a two-year-old Paint. Assuming it was Lily, he ignored it, continuing to the outside fence.

Whistling, Virgil caught Barrel's attention. Waving, the shorter man said something to the other ranch hands before joining Virgil.

"Owen, this is Barrel. You'll be sticking to him. He'll show you how we do things here at Whistle Rock Ranch. Our ways may be different from your experience, so pay attention. If you aren't sure about something, ask me or Barrel."

Owen gave a crisp nod. "Yes, sir."

"You have any questions for me, Barrel?"

"No, boss. I think me and Owen are going to get along just fine."

Whirling around, the amicable features fell from Virgil's face, replaced with a weary frown. Leaden feet guided him through the rest of the day, his heart heavy.

He didn't have dinner at the main house, deciding on scrambled eggs and toast. Taking a long shower, he slipped into sleeping pants before stretching out on his bed.

Lily didn't call again.

Lily had run out of ideas. After a dozen calls over a week, her hopes of talking with Virgil dissolved. She'd even spoken with Daisy, hoping Wyatt might encourage his friend to return her calls.

Harry had contacted her with news of Mason. The doctor continued to improve, though it would be several weeks before he'd be released into the care of his mother, who'd rarely left his side. Extensive physical therapy would follow. If all went well, Mason could return to his position at the hospital in six to eight months.

Her contact in human resources had called, asking if Lily still had an interest in the emergency department opening in Sheridan. The woman also mentioned a replacement for Mason had been selected, making Lily wonder if he'd have a job when he recovered from his injuries.

Each call made her wonder why she continued to wait for Virgil to reach out. It had taken him over eight years to make a move after ending their relationship in high school. How long would he wait this time?

Her heart ached at the division between them. She loved Virgil, wanted a future with him. How could they have a life together if he refused to speak to her?

Lily was approaching a time when a decision would have to be made. Stay in Brilliance and pray for the best, or forge a new future in Sheridan or Laramie.

"Do you remember the man I mentioned a few weeks ago who might be perfect for the new venture?" Wyatt stretched out on the front porch of the ranch house, a cold beer in his hand.

Virgil sat beside him, watching as three colts danced around each other in a nearby corral. "He never showed up for the interview."

"He called, asking me for another opportunity to interview. Seems his father had a major heart attack and he had to head home to Montana."

Tipping back the bottle, Virgil took a slow draw. "Do you believe he's worth it?"

"I do. That's why he's driving down next week."

"What about his father?"

Wyatt laughed at the antics in the corral. "Tucked away in a senior center with twenty-four hour care. We can confirm this if you believe he's a good fit."

"Why not? I haven't found anyone else and time is getting short. Let me know when he gets here."

"I know it's not my business."

"It's not."

Wyatt ignored the warning in Virgil's voice. "Have you spoken with Lily?"

Guilt ripped through him. As each day passed without returning her calls, Virgil sunk a little deeper into a hole of his own making. He ached to see her, hear her voice. Why couldn't he pick up the phone and call?

He knew the answer all too well. Virgil didn't want to hear her tell him she'd accepted a job and would be leaving.

"No."

"Is there a reason you haven't spoken to the woman you've been in love with most of your life?" Wyatt tipped his beer up for a deep swallow.

"My reasons are private."

"Since when? You've always talked about Lily with me."

"Since you married her best friend. I talk to you, it gets to Daisy, then to Lily."

Wyatt studied his best friend as if they hadn't known each other since they were five. "Are you interested in someone else?"

Virgil cast him a disbelieving look.

"Okay. Then what's the problem?"

Frustrated with Wyatt's continued questions, he grabbed another beer, removing the cap, and drinking half the contents. "She's still thinking about leaving. Until Lily makes a decision, I'm staying away."

"Did you ever think that might be why she's calling? Maybe she's made a decision and wants to share it." A light went on in Wyatt's mind, delivering a glint of understanding. "You're afraid she's decided to leave."

Virgil's throat worked as he continued to stare at the colts. Taking another draw from the bottle, he didn't respond.

"I've never known you to shy away from a difficult situation."

"Let it go, Wyatt," Virgil bit out.

"Fine." Rising, he stared down at the man who was more of a brother than a friend. "Don't let fear or pride contribute to you losing Lily. I guarantee you'll end up miserable and alone."

Chapter Twenty-Two

A loud knock on the apartment door woke Lily from a troubled sleep. Thinking she'd dreamed the loud noises, she rolled to her side, covering her face with a blanket.

"It's almost ten in the morning. I know you're in there, Lily. Open the door."

Sitting up, she stared toward the living room. Had she heard Virgil's voice? Rubbing sleep from her eyes, she shook her head, deciding she must've heard wrong. The knocking started again.

"Lily, if you don't open up, I'm going to use the key I know is under the pot on the porch."

It was Virgil. Scrambling, she grabbed a tank top and stabbed her legs into a pair of sweats in a heap on the floor. Checking the mirror, she ran fingers through the long strands, then rushed into the bathroom to brush her teeth.

The pounding started again. Slowing her pace and her breathing, she squared her shoulders before crossing the living room to the front door. Drawing it open, her heart tripped over itself at the sight of Virgil leaning against one of the posts.

"We need to talk." Before she could respond, he shoved the door wider and skirted past her, heading straight for the kitchen. Whirling around, he looked her up and down. "Guess I woke you up."

Ignoring her disgruntled expression, he brewed two cups of coffee. Stirring a little sugar and dollop of milk into each, he walked back to the living room. She hadn't moved from where he'd left her by the front door.

"You don't look so good."

Her expression flitted from irritated to hostile at his comment. "Yeah? Well, you woke me up."

"At ten in the morning. What's wrong? Not sleeping so well?" He held out a cup to her, which she ignored at first. "Take it or I'll drink it. So you know, I used the last two pods."

Taking the cup from his hand, she took a sip, her body relaxing a little at the comforting taste. "Why are you here?" Turning away, she lowered herself onto one of two overstuffed chairs, tucking both legs under her.

"Right to the point." He took the other chair, determined not to be rushed.

"I called at least a dozen times."

"I saw." Raising his cup, he took a few sips.

"Why didn't you call me back?"

"I wasn't ready."

"And now you are?"

"Yes."

A smug grin crossed her face. "What if I'm not ready?"

"Then I'll finish the coffee and leave. You can call me when you're ready."

Groaning in frustration, she set the cup down. "You are so irritating."

"It isn't intentional, Lily."

"Don't give me that. You don't breathe without thinking it through. Everything you do is intentional."

Forcing away a chuckle, he finished the coffee. "Get dressed. I'll take you to breakfast and we can talk."

Cocking a brow, she plastered him with a skeptical look. "Where?"

"For breakfast?"

She nodded.

"The Pancake Palace."

Stomach growling, she stood. Of course he'd pick her favorite spot. "Give me ten minutes."

"Take fifteen. They don't stop serving breakfast until two o'clock." He laughed when she sent him a withering glance before closing the bedroom door.

Allowing himself to breathe, he stood, opening the blinds to peer outside. He'd almost fallen off the porch when she opened the door in sweats, a tank top, and bare feet. Her hair was still mussed from sleep, her eyes glazed. Lily was stunningly beautiful. Even more so now than in high school.

Maturity had added curves to her slim body, and lines of wisdom to her face. How had some man not scooped her up during the years they were apart? Virgil knew the answer. It was the same reason he'd stayed single. He and Lily were meant to be together.

Hearing the bedroom door open, he turned from his spot by the window, once again stilling his reaction. She'd replaced the tank with a white blouse, adding white sandals. Her hair had been pulled into a ponytail. Except for lip gloss, she wore no makeup.

"I'm ready." Slinging her purse over a shoulder, she joined him by the door. "It's your party. Lead on."

Chuckling, he ushered her outside. Virgil had known the instant he awoke he'd be driving to town. Calling after so long didn't seem right. He had to face her, ask questions, and watch as she answered.

Walking to his truck, he didn't reach out to take her hand, making certain he stayed a good distance from her side. Touching Lily would create more of a connection than he wanted, and possibly lead to kissing. Until they sorted out their future, he meant to keep his desire well in check.

The Pancake Palace used to be where they'd go in high school. Open twenty-four hours a day, the food was good, plentiful, and cheap. Breakfasts of pancakes, eggs, and bacon were the best in a twenty mile radius. Families would stop in on Sundays after church, and teenagers filled the booths on Friday and Saturday nights.

Parking out front, Virgil jogged around the truck, opening the door to help Lily down. Again, he kept his distance, sitting across from her in a bright red vinyl booth. An older woman, with bleached blonde hair piled high on her head, walked toward them, carrying menus. Her eyes widened as she approached their table.

"Well, if it isn't Virgil and Lily. Haven't seen you two together since high school."

A broad smile blossomed across Virgil's face. "You're just as pretty as ever, Dottie."

"You always were a charmer. Now this one," she nodded at Lily, "comes in every few months with Daisy Raines. Well, it's Bonner now. So, what can I get you?"

Lily ordered her standard pancakes and a chocolate milkshake, eliciting a burst of laughter from Virgil. "Still the same."

She shrugged. "What can I say? It's what I like."

Ordering pancakes, eggs, bacon, and hash browns, Virgil relaxed in the booth, ready to get his questions answered. "Why were you calling me?"

"Why do you think? I wanted to talk."

"Must've been important. A dozen calls and eight voice messages. Those don't include the five texts."

They quieted while Dottie set plates and Lily's milkshake in front of them. Taking several bites of food, each watched the other until Virgil broke the silence. His deep, soft voice melted her defenses.

"Why'd you call me, Lily?"

Setting down her fork to lift the tall glass filled with chocolate shake, she sucked a mouthful through the straw. Letting the cold drink slide down her throat, she met his expectant gaze.

"I didn't appreciate the way you walked out on me at the restaurant. There were things we needed to discuss."

Chagrined, he shoved aside the guilt her words created. "You didn't think I'd be upset about your continued interest in job offers out of the area?"

Glancing away, Lily's throat tightened. "I shouldn't have mentioned it that night. We were there to celebrate the results of the tests. I'm sorry for that, Virgil."

"I was angry, Lily. Blindsided at your interest in leaving Brilliance. When I learned we weren't looking at the same future together, I had to get out of there."

Nodding, she lifted the shake glass, taking a long swallow. "I never said we didn't have a future."

"What did you expect would happen if you moved across state? If you're still considering leaving, I'm not interested in a long-distance relationship." When she didn't respond, he reached across the table, covering her hand with his. "I love you, Lily. There's never been anyone else for me. You need to be honest and tell me if you don't feel the same."

Lily already knew her answer. She'd known within minutes of him walking out of the restaurant.

"I've already called the hospitals and removed my name from consideration for any nursing position. My life is here in Brilliance. I want it to include you."

Virgil had no hesitation about holding Lily's hand as they walked to her front door. After her admission at the restaurant, he'd moved to sit next to her. They'd talked about moving forward over the next hour. Neither mentioned marriage. The focus remained on strengthening their relationship, rebuilding trust, and learning about each other as adults.

"Do you have time to come inside?"

"I do." Something weighed on Virgil. He hoped discussing it with Lily might bring some clarity.

"Would you like something to drink?"

"No, thanks." Lowering himself onto her sofa, he made no move to pull Lily closer when she sat near him. Staring at the backs of his hands, turning them over, he studied his palms, a haunted expression on his face.

"What is it, Virgil?"

"I'm trying to understand the relationship between my father and Monica. She contacted him about my uncle and your mother when she learned we were seeing each other. I believe they've been in contact ever since." He fell silent, looking again at his hands.

Reaching out, Lily placed her hand over one of his. "What is it that bothers you?"

Shifting to face her, Virgil rested an arm across the back of the sofa. "Why did she leave? What's the real reason she's here?"

"I thought you said it was her illness."

"That may be a small part of it. Other than fatigue, she has no symptoms."

"The medication has slowed its progress. Monica may still develop more symptoms over the years."

"I understand, Lily. But why come here? She doesn't need anyone to watch over her, as Jasper implied. She eats meals with him, and checks on him several times a day." Massaging the back of his neck, Virgil shook his head. "I believe she's here to make peace with Father, and somehow wrestle her way back into my life."

"Would that be so bad?"

"Yes." Rising, he paced to her bookcase, picking up a picture of the two of them at the cattle drive a few weeks earlier. He held it in the air. "This was the day Monica showed up. Father knew she was coming and said nothing to me. They've purposely left me out of everything." Virgil stared outside, not sure how to express the sense of deep betrayal.

He and Jasper were close, or had been until the last several months. Virgil wondered if it was because his parents began communicating more often.

Standing, Lily walked to him, threading her fingers with his. "You need to talk to them. Not just Jasper, but Monica too."

"I'm so angry with them."

"I know." She took his other hand in hers.

Focusing on their joined hands, Virgil met her encouraging gaze. "Will you be there with me?"

The question surprised her. This was a different Virgil than the self-assured man who faced problems head-on. The Virgil before her was achingly vulnerable.

"Yes. I'll go with you."

Chapter Twenty-Three

Virgil saw no reason to put off speaking with his father and Monica. He knew they'd be at the ranch. Jasper often took a nap after lunch. He had no idea what Monica did, although she did spend time with Margie working on items for the dude ranch.

He'd seen t-shirt samples showing the Whistle Rock Western Adventures name and logo. The staff would wear them, while others would be for sale to guests in the small gift shop.

Located in a new cabin constructed for use as a shop, it would offer clothing, jewelry, photography, pottery, and other goods by local artists. At least for the first year, most of the items would come from Daisy's store. He'd heard Monica would be the manager, which didn't thrill Virgil. Having her around bothered him on a level he couldn't describe.

With Lily by his side, they checked Jasper's apartment first. Finding it empty, they headed to the barn, then scanned the corrals.

"Hey, boss." Barrel tipped his hat at Lily. "Are you looking for Jasper?"

"I am. Do you know where he is?"

"Last I knew, he and Monica were meeting with Wyatt in the house. Wyatt tried to find you, but no one knew where you were." Barrel sent an apologetic glance at Lily. "They've been in there about half an hour."

"Thanks. How's Owen doing?"

"Great. He's smart, listens, watches the other men, and does his job. Owen's more comfortable around horses, but has worked with cattle. I'd love a few more like him."

"Do you think he'd be good on trail rides?"

Removing his hat, Barrel scratched his head. "Depends. He's pretty quiet. I don't know if it's from being shy, his time inside, or a little of both. The man is laid back, which might help the riders relax. I'd say try him on a few rides and see how he does."

"Good idea. I'm going to see if Wyatt still needs me in the meeting."

"Sounds good, boss. See you later, Lily."

Taking her hand, Virgil led them through the side door and to the office Wyatt shared with his mother. Lily pulled her hand from his.

"I'll stay out here."

"Wyatt isn't going to care if you're in there with me. Come on." Grabbing her hand again, he opened the door. "You were looking for me?"

"I was. Take a seat. We're talking about the gift shop." Seeing Lily, he grinned. "Hey. I didn't know you were on the ranch." Wyatt didn't miss their joined hands.

"I drove in with Virgil."

"Great. We can always use another opinion. Monica was sharing her thoughts on pricing."

Taking seats in the remaining chairs, Virgil grasped a set of stapled papers Wyatt held out. "Price sheets?"

Wyatt gave a sharp nod. "We're halfway through. Let's get this done."

An hour passed as they reviewed products and prices. Virgil thought the gift shop, while small, would be a success. He hadn't found a good reason to get behind Monica managing it. As the meeting broke up, he made the decision to keep his doubts to himself.

"Pop, do you and Monica have time to meet with Lily and me?"

"I do. Let me speak with Monica."

Lily slipped an arm through Virgil's, lowering her voice. "Do you know what you want to say?"

"I'm going to come right out and ask them why she left."

"Definitely to the point."

Virgil bent, brushing a kiss across her lips, lifting his head as Jasper returned.

"Monica has time. Where do you want to talk?"

"If you're okay with it, the apartment is fine."

"Fine with me."

The four walked to the back of the bunkhouse, where Jasper's apartment was located. With Virgil now staying in one of the cabins, his father had the space to himself.

Shoving the door open, Jasper motioned the others inside. "I can make coffee, or there's a case of water in the refrigerator."

Virgil grabbed four bottles, placing them on the small dining table with two chairs.

"Jasper and I can sit on the bed." Monica picked up a bottle of water and sat down. Jasper joined her, while Virgil and Lily took the chairs.

"What did you want to talk about?" Jasper twisted off the top, drinking a third of the contents.

Virgil glanced at his father before spearing Monica with hard, chocolate-brown eyes so much like his own. "Why did you leave?"

Her lips parted on a sharp intake of breath.

"What kind of question is that?" Jasper's voice was as steely as Virgil's.

"It's a fair question, Pop."

Jasper's mouth tightened as the color leached from his face. He looked as if he was going to lose whatever he'd eaten for lunch.

Knocking over the chair as he stood, Virgil rushed to his father's side. "Pop. Are you all right?"

"He will be." Monica shifted on the bed, taking Jasper's hand. "Give him a few minutes."

Frantic eyes met his mother's. "What's wrong with him?"

Jasper bent a few inches at the waist, his breaths coming in short gasps. Long moments passed before he straightened, color returning to his face.

"You'll understand once we explain why I left." Monica cupped Jasper's cheek. "We have to tell him, my love."

Jasper locked gazes with Virgil. "I should've told you years ago."

Moving back to his chair, Virgil slid it closer to Lily, taking her hand in his. "Take all the time you need."

"First, what happened between your mother and me was my fault."

Virgil's eyes flashed for an instant before narrowing on his father. "All right."

"Monica and I began to have problems soon after your fourth birthday. She wanted to train horses. The same as you, she had a gift." Jasper looked at Monica. "Still has a gift. But I was stubborn, determined to be the one who supported the family. I wanted more children. A passel of them is what we talked about before we married. I've always been old-fashioned. We began to argue."

Lifting the bottle to his lips, he swallowed several large gulps. "Several months went by with us going to bed angry each night. We hardly spoke. When we did, it deteriorated into us yelling, blaming the other for our problems."

Scrubbing a hand down his face, Jasper stood, pacing to the window. "Storm's coming." He shook his head. "Anyway, one night, it got particularly bad. We said horrible things to each other. When I couldn't hear anymore, I grabbed the keys to the truck and left."

"Left?" Virgil remembered times when they argued, but was too young to understand the fallout.

"I didn't have anywhere specific in mind. Driving around the reservation, I tried to clear the anger from my mind. After a while, I found myself parked in front of the home of my old girlfriend. We'd been together for two years before I met your mother. About the same time, my girlfriend met someone else too. The split was amicable. I knew she hadn't married. The word was she was seeing one of the tribal police officers." He turned away, placing his hands on the counter, lowering his head.

"I made the biggest mistake of my life and knocked on her door."

Pressing palms against his eyes, Virgil expelled a deep sigh.

Monica joined Jasper at the counter, placing a hand on his shoulder before turning her attention to Virgil. "I took you to the neighbor's and borrowed her car. It took a while before figuring out where he might've gone. Sure enough, his truck was outside his ex-girlfriend's place. Instead of going home, waiting for him to explain, I waited in my car across the street. At five o'clock in the morning, just when the sun began to show, he walked out her front door. As you'd expect, I jumped to conclusions, didn't let Jasper explain. All those years lost because of assumptions."

Virgil's focus moved between Monica and Jasper. "What do you mean?"

"My ex and I talked for hours. I fell asleep on her sofa. We didn't sleep together. Monica didn't learn this until years later."

"Jasper didn't see me when he climbed into the truck after leaving her house. I dashed home, picked you up at the neighbor's, and went to bed. My entire world had collapsed in a few short hours. Jasper came home, but didn't climb into bed. He took a shower and headed to work. While he was gone, I packed my clothes, and yours, Virgil. Someone must've seen me loading my car and called Jasper."

Monica leaned into Jasper's side, closing her eyes. Placing an arm around her waist, he tugged her close.

"I left work and returned home. The blowup was horrific. We were screaming at each other while not hearing a word the other said. And, Virgil, you were standing to the side, your hands over your ears. The neighbor lady took you to her house. Monica was determined to leave, and planned to take you with her. I forbade it. Told her she could leave, that I wouldn't miss her. But there was no way I'd let her leave with you."

Jumping to his feet, Virgil stepped behind Lily's chair, resting his hands on the back. He wasn't prepared for the tears burning at the back of his eyes. All these years, he blamed his mother, believed she'd walked out on them. On him.

"Being on the rez," Jasper continued, "we were subject to tribal law. We took it to the council. They listened to your mother, then to me. The truth is, I always knew they'd never let her leave with you, Virgil. If Monica wanted to leave the rez, no one would stop her. She wasn't allowed to take you. The council encouraged her to leave, take time away to let things settle between us. I, well...didn't try to stop her. I threw her bags into the car and told her not to return."

"I called often, but Jasper wouldn't allow me to speak with you, Virgil. He refused to let me see you. He wouldn't even consider meeting off the rez at a neutral location. There were many times I'd sit in my car, watching those leaving the rez, hoping for a glimpse of you." Monica swiped at a tear, then another. "I lived less than a mile away until Jasper brought you to Whistle Rock Ranch. It took a long time to find work, but eventually, a rancher south of Brilliance hired me to train horses and be the ranch cook. I'd often watch you from various spots around the ranch. My mistake was not going after my parental rights when you moved to Wyoming."

"What Monica isn't saying," Jasper added, "is she had no money for an attorney. She satisfied herself with occasional sightings of you."

Virgil felt ill. Stumbling to the door, he drew it open, in desperate need of fresh air.

Lily stared after him, stricken at the pain his parents caused their son. He'd gone through most of his life believing Monica didn't want him. The opposite was true.

196

When Monica disappeared into the bathroom, Lily stepped outside to join Virgil. He leaned against the outside wall, hands in pockets, staring at the ground. She didn't speak when stopping beside him. They stood there for long minutes before he reached out to take her hand.

"This isn't what I expected. I don't know what to do with what they've told me."

"There's nothing you have to do. At least not right away. None of what happened between them was because of you. You're blameless in all of this."

Virgil didn't reply as he continued to wrestle with what he'd learned. It had been a long time since she'd witnessed such misery on his face.

"I need to get away from here. Do you want to go with me?" He squeezed her hand.

Nodding, she kissed his cheek. "Just try to leave without me."

Chapter Twenty-Four

Virgil drove for an hour. Neither spoke, although Lily could almost hear the internal conversation churning inside his head. She hadn't scooted next to him, nor had he reached for her hand. He'd give her a sign when he wanted her closer.

Turning into a campground, both waved at the ranger who'd attended high school with them. Virgil followed the narrow drive, parking in a shaded spot with an amazing view of the crystalline lake.

Shutting off the engine threw them into almost total silence. The occasional sound of a bird, or laughter from a nearby campsite, was all that broke the quiet.

Lily didn't know how much time passed before he reached over to grab her hand. "It's hard for me to reconcile the man who raised me to the one Jasper and Monica described. He's never yelled at me in anger. The one time he was implacable was when he forbade me from seeing you."

Tugging her close, he placed an arm over her shoulder, tucking her into his side. "The man I've looked up to my entire life kept Monica away from me for over twenty years. Why would he do that?"

She didn't respond, knowing answers to his questions could only come from Jasper or Monica. Resting her head against his shoulder, she watched a bird dip to the lake. Rising, it's wings flapping, she saw the fish snug in the bird's beak. A reminder of how life could change in less than a heartbeat.

Lily wondered if either Jasper or Monica considered how their rash actions had impacted their five-year-old son. She knew Virgil had longed for his mother, never understanding how she could've walked out of his life without a backward glance.

As painful as the truth was to hear, it helped answer many of Virgil's questions. At twenty-eight, he could begin the hard process of dealing with what he'd learned.

"Did you hear them mention divorce?"

Virgil stilled at Lily's question. "No. Jasper's never said if they got one. Why?"

"Curiosity. I was wondering if they were still married."

"I've never thought about it. It wouldn't surprise me if they are." He kissed the top of her head. "What a mess." A moment later, Virgil chuckled. "I might be the only person who sees it that way."

"A mess?"

"Yeah. Jasper and Monica have been living with their breakup for years. Wouldn't surprise me if they've been seeing each other since she moved to Brilliance. My mother has been less than half an hour away, and I never knew it. She could've been a part of my life. Jasper should've made it happen. He should've..." Virgil stopped at the catch in his voice.

His grip on her shoulders tightened as he brought himself under control.

Lily set a hand on his knee. "You know, it's all right to cry."

A burst of shaky laughter filled the truck. "Me cry?" But the tone of his voice said something else.

She shifted closer to him when the sound of a quiet sob hit her. Rising, Lily rested on her knees, wrapping both arms around him as another sob broke loose.

The pitch black of a moonless night greeted Virgil when he walked Lily to her front door. He'd love to stretch out on her sofa and stay the night. Anything was preferable to driving back to his cabin on the ranch, where he knew Jasper and Monica would want to continue their conversation.

"Why don't you come inside for coffee before heading back to the ranch?" Lily's hand pressed against his. He hadn't let go since they'd left the campground. "You can also sleep on the sofa if you're not ready to face your parents."

"You have no idea how tempting staying at your place sounds." He followed her inside, still keeping a grip on her hand.

"I know the sofa is a little short for you. I could take it and you could use my bed."

"I'm not taking your bed, Lily. I'll stay a while, then I need to head back." Wrapping his arms around her, he drew her in for a long, deep kiss.

By the time he lifted his head, both were breathing heavily. Unable to stop himself, he captured her mouth again. Tasting every recess, his tongue sent shudders of desire rippling through her.

She returned his kiss, passion roaring through her. Burning for him, her fingers dug into his shoulder, a moan escaping her lips.

Lifting his head, he rested his forehead against hers, doing his best to calm his raging need for this woman.

"Marry me, Lily." He swept her into his arms, lowering himself onto the sofa so she laid snug against his chest.

"What?" She giggled at his antics.

"Marry me. Soon. Tomorrow, if you can get off work." Pressing his mouth against hers, he crushed her against him.

She pushed against his shoulder, lifting her mouth from his. "Why?"

Brows drawing together, he couldn't hide his confusion. "Why?"

"Why the rush?"

"Does that mean you will marry me?"

"Of course I'm going to marry you. I just thought we were going to take our time."

Placing a hand at the back of her neck, he brought her toward him for another searing kiss. Savoring her taste, he closed his eyes, heart pounding in his chest.

"I love you, Lily. You're it for me. If you feel the same, let's get married."

Searching his face, seeing the sincerity in his eyes, Lily's heart melted. "All right."

"All right?"

"I love you, Virgil. I'll marry you whenever you're ready."

"Tomorrow. We'll meet at the county clerk's office at three o'clock. I'll bring Wyatt. You bring Daisy."

Lips parting, her eyes widened. "You're serious."

"Never more so."

Her mind spun at the commitment he wanted. She'd known Virgil the majority of her life. Loved him just as long. Though sudden, she couldn't argue with her heart.

"If you're certain. There can't be any regrets."

"No regrets, sweetheart. By tomorrow night, you'll be Mrs. Lily Redstar."

Cupping her face in his hands, he gave her the sweetest kiss they'd ever shared.

Lily found it hard to concentrate. She'd gotten less than three hours sleep, her mind stuck on the events of today. After all the pain, the years of separation, she and Virgil were getting married.

They'd spoken several times since not long after sunup. He'd made all the arrangements. A friend of his and an associate pastor at their church had agreed to meet them at a small park in town at four o'clock, giving them plenty of time to complete the marriage application. Wyatt and Daisy had agreed to meet at the park, although they didn't know why. Afterward, the four would go to the steakhouse for an early dinner.

Lily had been surprised when her boss had granted her the afternoon off. When she'd told him the reason, he'd insisted she take an extra day.

She hadn't been able to keep any food down all day. Her biggest fear was fainting from hunger during the ceremony. It made her wonder how Virgil was doing. Probably fine. Nothing much rattled him. Until yesterday.

Learning the real reason behind his parents' separation had cut deep. She suspected it would take time to get past the hurt Jasper and Monica had created by their selfish actions.

By two o'clock, her body hummed with stress-filled excitement. In fifteen minutes, she'd disappear into the employee lounge to change clothes. There'd been no time to buy a special outfit for the wedding.

Virgil had been wonderful, telling Lily she could wear jeans and a tank top. It didn't matter to him. What mattered was the two of them joining their lives after being in love since their teens.

Before leaving her house, she'd questioned him about inviting Jasper and Monica. He'd been adamant about keeping the wedding small. She believed it had more to do with his unsettled feelings about his parents.

Seeing the clock strike two-twenty, she ducked into the lounge, removing a small bag from her locker. It took little time to slip into the red sundress with tiny white and yellow flowers. Her white sandals were perfect, as was the lightweight white swing jacket.

A little mascara and lip gloss came next. Adding a pair of tiny gold earrings, the ones Virgil had given the Christmas before he left for college, she checked the mirror. Casual would work just fine to marry the love of her life, she decided.

Stuffing her nursing uniform into the almost empty bag, she glanced around. Lily slid her purse onto a shoulder, picked up the bag, and started for the hall. In ten minutes, she'd enter the county clerk's office, completing paperwork which would change her life.

Before she could reach it, the door to the lounge blew open, one of her coworkers coming to a halt. "Lily..."

After a moment, she stepped to the other nurse. "What is it?"

"You're wanted in emergency. Stat."

Glancing down at her clothes, she tossed her purse into the locker, rummaged for her practical shoes, and hurried down the hall. The scene before her had Lily coming to an abrupt stop.

Outside one of the emergency cubicles stood Monica and Virgil. Their stricken faces told her something was very wrong.

Stepping to Virgil, he wrapped arms around her. "It's Jasper. We think he's having a heart attack."

Chapter Twenty-Five

Lily stepped out of Virgil's embrace. "You won't be able to stay here. Why don't you locate chairs in the waiting room while I find out what's going on? I'll join you as soon as possible."

"You're right. Come on, Monica." Virgil placed a hand on his mother's back, guiding her toward the waiting area. "Come find us if...well, just come find us, Lily."

"I will." Waiting until they'd gone through the door, she slipped into a gown, scrubbing her hands and arms before rushing to Jasper's cubicle. Sliding back the curtain, Lily watched the controlled chaos created by three professionals working over a distressed patient.

"What can I do?"

The doctor didn't glance up as the team worked to stabilize Jasper. "Acute asthma attack. I want you to stay with the family."

Lightly placing a hand on the top of Jasper's head, she bent down, hoping he'd hear her. "It's Lily, Jasper. You're going to be fine. Stay calm and relax. Let the doctor work his magic."

His eyes flickered, letting Lily know Jasper could hear her. She didn't know how much he understood.

Giving a brisk nod to the doctor, she took one more look at Jasper before leaving to join Virgil and Monica. Entering the waiting area, she spotted them right away. The group had increased to include Anson, Margie, Wyatt, and Daisy. Virgil saw her first, covering the distance between them in seconds.

"How is he?"

"The doctor will come out to talk to us after Jasper is stabilized."

"Was it a heart attack?" Monica wrapped both arms around her waist.

"I really shouldn't say what I think."

"Lily. Please. What happened?" There were increased lines around Monica's eyes and mouth. She appeared close to collapsing.

Sighing, she ushered them to a quiet corner. "First, tell me what happened leading up to when Jasper arrived at the hospital."

Virgil gave his mother a reassuring look. Monica let out a shaky breath, grasping both hands in her lap.

"Jasper had finished lunch. He decided to lunge one of the young horses. I stayed in the apartment to work on the product list for the gift shop. About thirty minutes went by before I set the work aside to watch him. I saw Jasper pull his inhaler from a pocket. I knew it had to be his asthma. He took a few puffs, but it was clear the asthma wasn't letting up." Monica's gaze moved across the room to where a young couple were arguing. She noticed the man had a gash on his forehead.

"Monica?"

"Sorry, Lily. Anyway, the horse continued lunging another minute or so before Jasper began to fold into himself and crumbled to the ground. Barrel and I ran into the pen at the same time. He picked up the lunge line, and took control of the horse while I checked on Jasper. His breath was coming in gasps. He was able to tell me he couldn't breathe."

Monica pressed fingers to her temples. "I yelled at Barrel to call 9-1-1. Jasper's color began to change. I tried to get him to use the inhaler again, but he shook his head, giving me the impression it wasn't working. He was in agony. I was so scared. Barrel ran back to me, the phone at his ear. He helped me lay Jasper down so I could perform CPR. By some miracle, the EMTs came roaring onto the ranch, parking right by the corral. Turned out the EMTs were returning to the hospital from a false alarm and were just passing the ranch. It's all a blur after that." She began to sway. Virgil's hand shot out to steady her.

"Sit down, Monica. I'll get you some water." Virgil walked to a machine to purchase a bottle of water. "Here."

After several sips, she returned her attention to Lily. "I got in the back of the ambulance with Jasper. Virgil saw the commotion and followed us in his truck."

Virgil shifted toward Lily. "What do you think?"

Lily sat next to him, waiting as the others pulled chairs up to form a circle. "This is my personal opinion based on what you've said. The doctor hasn't told me anything, so I may be way off. It seems Jasper had an acute asthma attack, which resulted in him not being able to breathe, causing his heart to stop. CPR and the quick arrival of the EMTs may have saved his life."

"It makes sense," Monica said. "The EMTs used the defibrillator."

"Lily?"

The doctor stopped next to her. "Is this the family?"

"Yes, doctor. Monica Redstar and her son, Virgil. This is Doctor Ryan."

"We've been able to stabilize Mr. Redstar. An acute asthma attack caused his heart to stop. He's on medications. At a minimum, I'd like to keep him overnight. Does he have a history of heart disease?"

Virgil shook his head. "No. The asthma issue is new, also. We're still figuring out how to deal with it."

"I'm going to refer Mr. Redstar to an asthma and allergy specialist in Jackson. I'd advise getting an appointment soon after he's released from the hospital. Was he doing something strenuous when the attack occurred?"

"Jasper was lunging a horse," Monica answered.

"Hmmm. Well, that's not too arduous. The dirt in the air may have triggered the attack. Sometimes, we aren't able to pinpoint the exact cause. Do you have any questions?"

"Will there be any special instructions or restrictions?" Virgil asked.

"Yes. I'll have them ready for you, along with some updated medications when he's released. Lily knows how to reach me if there are additional questions."

Ryan accepted Virgil's outstretched hand. "Thank you, doctor."

Virgil and Monica stayed at the hospital with Lily until Jasper had been moved to a private room. The Bonners left after Virgil promised to call if there was any change in Jasper's condition.

It took until eleven that night for Jasper to be moved. They visited for a short time before the drugs took over and Jasper drifted off.

"I'm going to stay." Monica pulled the only comfortable chair next to the bed, tucking her feet beneath her.

"You'll be all right?" Virgil grabbed a blanket from a shelf, handing it to Monica.

"I'll be fine. You go on. I'll see you in the morning. Bring coffee."

"I will. In case you need to leave, these are the keys to my truck." Laying them on a table, he took Lily's hand.

Neither spoke as they walked through the almost empty hall to the elevator and on to her car. Too tired to stop anywhere, they poured cereal and milk into bowls, relaxing on the sofa while watching an old western.

With his arm draped over her shoulders, he tucked Lily close. "I'm sorry about putting off the wedding."

"You have no reason to be sorry, Virgil. I'm just thankful Jasper reached the hospital in time."

"We almost lost him."

"But you didn't. You're fortunate. Jasper has another chance. So do you and Monica. Many people don't have such an opportunity."

He kissed her forehead. "You never had the chance with your parents."

"The car accident took the choice from me." Her parents had died in an accident on the way to her college graduation. She looked up into his face, accepting the kiss when he lowered his head.

Sliding a hand behind his neck, she held him in place. The kiss continued, both gasping for air when Virgil lifted his head, his gaze holding hers.

"We'll marry as soon as my father returns to the ranch."

She thought of the red sundress on the floor of her bedroom. Wrinkled from a day spent waiting for word on Jasper, it would need to be washed before rescheduling their wedding.

"Are you certain you don't want a big wedding, Lily?"

"My family will be there. You, Wyatt, and Daisy. You're my family."

Kissing her nose, he hugged her against him, knowing what a blessing he held in his arms. "Then we'll have a reception. Margie and Monica would love to do that for us."

"You don't think they'll be against our marriage?"

"Why would they? Margie's wanted us to reconcile for years. Monica already cares a great deal about you. She's not going to oppose us marrying."

Her frown didn't disappear. "What of Jasper?"

"Father still deals with the guilt of not explaining the reason for his order years ago. I've told him we can't go back, only forward, assuring him neither of us are angry with him. Our biggest problem will be having enough food for all our friends who want to celebrate with us."

A soft chuckle burst from her, lessening the worry over Jasper's condition.

"Once we're married, I want you to live with me in the cabin until we build our house."

"We might have to enlarge the closet." There was a smile in her voice.

"You're right." He kissed the tip of her nose. "We'll draw up house plans when you move to the ranch."

"I have money saved. I can help pay for our house."

"I don't need your money, Lily."

The crisp response surprised her. "I'm sure you don't. What if I want to help?"

Virgil fell silent, his soft breaths playing across her face. "I've lived with my father all my life. Most of it in the apartment. Anson supplied what little furniture there is."

Sitting up, excitement clung to her. "Wonderful. I'll buy the furniture."

"Hold on, sweetheart. I don't want all that flowery stuff you have in your apartment."

Gently shoving his shoulder, she smiled. "There are a lot more choices than flowers."

"I get veto power." Virgil's voice had turned surly.

"Daisy will want to help pick everything out."

"I'm sure she will," he mumbled, too low for Lily to hear.

"What?"

"Remember, she'll be busy buying furniture for her house."

"Even better. We can plan together."

Virgil cringed. He could almost see his new house decked out in yellows, blues, whites, and oranges. Flowered pillows on the sofas and beds. His stomach hurt thinking about it.

Closing his eyes, he went to sleep with visions of giant sunflowers laughing at him.

Chapter Twenty-Six

"Virgil?" Lily hated to wake him so early. She'd heard him shuffling about after retreating into her bedroom.

"Virgil?" She gave his shoulder a shake.

"What?" He sat up, at first not knowing where he was. Then he remembered. Lily's sofa.

"Monica called. The doctor wants to keep Jasper most of today. There are more tests he wants to run."

"What time is it?"

"Almost seven."

Swinging his feet to the ground, he stood. "Can't believe I slept this late. I'd better call Wyatt."

"I already did. He figured you wouldn't be at the ranch today."

"I put towels in the bathroom, along with deodorant, a toothbrush, and paste. You can use my brush." His long, black hair had come loose from the tie. Falling halfway down his back, it was longer than Lily's.

"Thanks. I won't take long. We need to stop for coffee."

"I called Lydia. She'll have three coffees ready when we stop in."

He lifted a brow. "Plus bear claws?"

"And scones and croissants."

"I love you, Lily."

"Yeah. I know."

Laughing, he grabbed his socks and boots before heading to the bathroom. She knew he wouldn't take long.

Sitting down at the dining room table, she checked messages. Two new ones from hospitals had arrived, both requesting a phone interview. She politely declined each one.

Good to her word, Lydia had two bags of pastries and three coffees ready to go. "I'll put it on Lily's tab," Lydia told Virgil when he went to pull out his wallet. "Works better for both of us. Plus, we visit over coffee and cake when she comes in to pay."

Shaking his head, he picked up the tray of drinks, joining Lily at the door. "Those are pretty big bags for three people."

Holding them up, Lily had to agree. "I told her Jasper wouldn't be going home until later today, or maybe tomorrow. Lydia didn't want us to run out."

They reached the hospital in less than five minutes. Monica sat in the same chair, talking with Jasper as he ate breakfast.

"Good morning. How are you feeling, Pop?"

"Better. I don't know why they need more tests. This food is..." Jasper looked at Lily. "It could be better."

"Don't I know it." Lily pulled two straight back chairs with thin padding on the seats toward the bed. "Eat what you can."

Virgil set coffee on the table by his mother, and opened the bags. "Lydia sent an assortment of pastries." He pulled out a bear claw for himself and raspberry scone for Lily. "There's plenty." Handing the bag to Monica, he set his and Lily's pastries on napkins. "I don't think they're on your diet, Pop."

"I don't care about their diet. What do you have in there?"

Lily shot a look at Virgil. "Well, there might be a biscuit with egg at the bottom of one bag."

"Lydia's?" Jasper asked.

"Of course."

"Hand it over, son."

Digging into the bag, Virgil pulled out a warm, separately wrapped item. "This must be it."

Jasper reached for it. "Hurry before the nurse comes back. She's a real ball bu..." Again, he looked at Lily. "The woman scares me."

"She scares me too. But she's the law on this floor." Lily bit into her scone, humming with pleasure. "Lydia makes the best scones. Wish she'd share the recipe."

"Maybe Margie has it. They're good friends." Finishing his bear claw, Virgil reached into the same sack. This time, he pulled out a chocolate croissant.

"Nope. Lydia turned Margie down when she asked."

"I haven't met her." Monica wiped her hands on a napkin. When Virgil held up the sack, she shook her head.

Lily swallowed coffee, setting the cup down. "If you stay, I'll introduce you. She owns Brilliance Coffee &

Bakery. Lydia's real nice, but no-nonsense when it comes to her business. I'm pretty sure she keeps her recipes locked in a safe. She opened a shop in Jackson. It was an immediate success."

"Who runs it?" Monica chuckled when Jasper stuffed the last of the biscuit into his mouth.

"She hired a man with a pastry degree from some well-known school. He grew up somewhere in Wyoming. I've never met him, but Margie says he's a real hottie." Lily grinned when Virgil choked on his coffee.

"Maybe we should drive over there with Daisy and check it out for ourselves." Monica didn't mean it as a question.

"Great idea. I'll talk to Daisy about it." Wadding up her napkin, Lily tossed it into the nearby receptacle. "I'm stuffed."

"Well, Mr. Redstar. I see you've attracted quite a following." A tall, reed-thin nurse stepped into the room. Lily didn't know Rochelle's age, guessing her to be around forty.

"If it isn't my favorite nurse." Jasper's forced grin was at odds with the greeting.

Rochelle began checking his vitals, spotting a few crumbs of food on his gown. "You aren't eating anything you shouldn't, are you?"

"You were quite clear on what I could and couldn't eat."

Hearing the non-answer, Lily stepped next to her. "When have the tests been scheduled?"

"Anytime now. More blood work and an MRI." Finishing, Rochelle sent a withering look at Jasper.

"No more pastries until you go home, Mr. Redstar. Understand?" She flicked a glance at Lily, winking.

"I didn't—"

Rochelle held up her hand. "That's all I have to say on the subject. Be good for the techs when they take you for tests."

Lily bit her bottom lip so as not to chuckle. If she didn't know better, she'd think Rochelle was flirting with Jasper.

The nurse hadn't been gone a minute when a pair of technicians arrived. The younger of the two smiled. "Hey, Lily. Haven't seen you in a while."

"I transferred to emergency not long ago."

He continued as they transferred Jasper onto the gurney. "That's probably the reason. We should meet for lunch sometime. You know. To catch up."

Virgil stood, watching them move his father while snaking an arm around Lily's waist. The gesture wasn't lost on the young man. He looked at Virgil.

"Sorry, man. Didn't know Lily was tied up."

"Now you do. This is my father. How long until you bring him back?"

"There isn't much activity in imaging. An hour, maybe."

"Thanks." Virgil took Jasper's hand. "We'll be here when you get back."

"Save me one of those pastries."

"No promises, Pop." He chuckled at his father's scowl. Once his father was in the elevator, he turned to Lily. "Who's the pup?"

"He's harmless and very good at his job."

"Which is?"

"Imaging technician. I don't know why he's transporting patients. He's usually too busy. What would you like to do for an hour?"

Virgil's phone chimed before he could respond. "Hold on, Lily. It's Wyatt." He walked into the hall.

"Were you able to sleep last night, Monica?"

Shoving herself out of the chair, she stretched. "Some. I don't know how many times the nurse came in to check on him, but it was a lot. You just get back to sleep, and someone else would come in. It didn't seem to bother Jasper. He hardly stirred."

"He's in good spirits."

"Yes, he is. Do you and Virgil plan to marry?"

The sudden change of subject surprised Lily. "Yes. I do believe we'll marry."

"Good. The two of you make a strong couple." Monica leaned against the bed, clasping her hands together. "I'm sure you're thinking I know little about Virgil."

"Not really. I do believe you and Virgil need time to be comfortable around each other."

Monica looked away, as if uncomfortable. "I do love him."

"Virgil loves you too."

"Do you truly think so?"

"Yes, I do. He was deeply hurt when you left and never returned. Learning Jasper played a big part in your separation hit him hard. It's as if all he knew was a lie. Give him time."

Virgil walked back into the room, pocketing his phone while looking between the two women. "Graduation ceremonies for Jonah and Gage are next Friday. Wyatt wanted to know if you and I are interested in going. I told him it depends on Jasper."

"I'll be here with him if you two want to go."

Virgil studied his mother, trying to figure her out. Not once had she apologized to him for leaving. What kind of mother leaves her five-year-old son and doesn't return? Knowing the reason gave him no comfort. She'd been living in the area since soon after he and Jasper had moved to Brilliance. Why had she never sought him out?

Turning away, he shifted his focus to Lily. "Are you interested?"

"If I can get the time off, yes."

"Let me know if you can. I need to make another call." Bending down, he kissed her, uncaring that Monica watched. He left the room, never acknowledging his mother's offer to stay with Jasper.

Jasper was returned to the room while Virgil made his call. Though still in good spirits, his face was drawn, the earlier spark in his eyes dimmed.

Once the three were alone, Lily stepped next to the bed. "You look tired."

"I'm ready to get out of this place." Jasper rested his head against the pillow and closed his eyes.

The doctor visited before Virgil returned. He explained the results of the tests and MRI, discussed asthma triggers and confirmed Jasper would keep his inhaler with him at all times. Flu and pneumonia shots were ordered before Jasper could be discharged.

The concerning part was the instructions regarding environmental triggers. He was to avoid work or leisure activities where dust was prevalent. The doctor cautioned him about grooming the horses, recommending someone else handle the job. Smoking, or being around anyone who smoked, was discouraged.

Before leaving, he explained the additional medications ordered. Virgil returned as the doctor finished with the warning signs of another possible acute asthma attack.

Virgil pushed the wheelchair to the entrance, leaving Jasper with Monica and Lily while he fetched the truck. Not once did Virgil talk directly to Monica or meet her gaze.

He couldn't get past the knowledge his mother lived within thirty minutes of him for over twenty years and never once sought him out.

Chapter Twenty-Seven

"Why are you doing this to her, Virgil?" Lily finished cinching Jiminy's saddle in preparation for their ride. "Anyone can see how upset she is by the way you ignore her."

Grabbing Migisi's reins, his black and white Paint mare lifted her head in an excited whinny. "Of everyone, I thought you'd understand."

It had been three days since Jasper left the hospital, and Lily couldn't get Monica's abject disappointment out of her mind. Virgil had deliberately ignored his mother, treating her as if she didn't exist. His attitude toward her was so out of character, it worried Lily.

She'd been in Jasper's living quarters when he and Monica confessed the truth about their breakup. Lily felt little except sorrow for them and Virgil.

"You treat Jasper as if he played no part in the separation. Your mother, who might be less to blame, endures your contempt. Why, Virgil?"

Assisting her into the saddle, Virgil mounted Migisi, reining her north. They rode for ten minutes before Lily pulled up beside him.

"Are you going to answer me?"

"Not yet."

She bit off a response, his answer not appeasing her. They rode past the cabins built for the new venture. In a few weeks, they'd be filled with the ranch's first customers, people who chose to have a true western experience.

Daisy had carved out a place for herself in the endeavor, supplying photography, jewelry, and pottery for the gift shop. Monica would be managing it, while Margie was the overall administrator.

When she and Virgil married, Lily would play no part. Her work at the hospital would require her absence a good deal of the time. Daisy had invited her to participate in the trail rides, which she intended to do.

Continuing along a trail she'd never ridden, Lily again thought of Monica, and the rift between her and Virgil. She wondered if marriage to a man who couldn't forgive his mother was wise. For a moment, she forgot about her deep love for Virgil, all the good qualities which had drawn her to him as a child and also as an adult.

An hour passed before they stopped next to one of several creeks running through the ranch. This one seemed familiar. Had he brought her out here to fish?

"I can see you remember this place." Virgil held out his hands to help her to the ground. He knew it wasn't necessary. It had been several days since they'd seen each other, and he couldn't wait another second to feel her near him. Bending, he kissed her. Meant as a quick peck, it turned heated as their mouths melded together. Knowing she wanted to talk, he lifted his head.

"I've wanted to do that since you arrived at the ranch."

"You could've kissed me then." She ground tied Jiminy and looked around.

"Waiting until we were alone was better. So, do you remember fishing here?"

"I do. It hasn't changed much."

He took her hand, the warmth of her skin calming him as they walked to the creek. "I've come here many times over the years. Never catch much." He shrugged, chuckling. "The fact is, I've caught one fish in all these years. If I remember right, I tossed him back."

Sitting down on the bank, he tugged her down next to him. "I don't know what to do about Monica."

Lily was glad she didn't have to bring up his mother. "Have you forgiven Jasper for what happened?"

The question surprised him. "What else could I do? He's my father. The man who raised me."

"Yet you can't forgive Monica?"

Virgil watched the creek flow, catching in an eddy before moving on. "I don't know. She lived near Brilliance for twenty years and never tried to contact me."

"How do you know?"

He shot her a confused look. "What do you mean?"

"Monica also told us Jasper wouldn't allow her to see you."

"I've thought of that."

"What conclusion did you come to?"

"I haven't."

"Is avoidance your answer until you figure out what to do about her?"

Grasping a rock, he tossed it into the creek. "My intention isn't to hurt her."

"Are you sure? Each time you pass Monica without acknowledging her is a painful reminder of all she lost. It wasn't her choice to leave you behind."

"I know." He pulled the leather thong from his hair, allowing the long, black locks to flow in the breeze. Reaching out, he placed a hand on her knee. "We leave in three days for the graduation. I want to be married before we leave."

Lily considered the timing, as well as the issue with Monica. "All right. But I'd ask you to first make things right with Monica."

His head whipped toward her. "Before we marry?"

"I don't believe I'm asking too much."

Tossing his hair behind him, Virgil tied it with the leather band before standing. Reaching out, he helped her up, then gripped her shoulders.

"You're saying you won't marry me until I've made peace with Monica?"

"I'd prefer not to start our life together with animosity between the two of you."

Closing his eyes, he wrapped his arms around her, resting his chin on the top of her head. "I'll take care of it."

True to his word, the instant they returned to the ranch, untacked and groomed the horses, he sought out his mother. Unsurprising, he found her in a chair next to Jasper's bed, reading while his father slept.

Doing his best not to wake him, he stopped behind Monica. "Do you have a few minutes to talk?"

Setting the book down, she stood. "We can't talk in here without waking him."

"We'll find a place in the house." Stepping outside, he grabbed Lily's hand.

Monica didn't seem shocked to see her when joining them. Whenever she'd seen Lily at the ranch, Virgil wasn't too far away. Much as she and Jasper had been before they married.

Finding the office Wyatt used empty, Virgil closed the door behind them. He didn't wait until Monica sat down.

"Why didn't you ever come for me?"

Stilling at the accusation in her son's voice, she had a hard time holding his hard gaze. "I tried half a dozen times. Jasper, Anson, or one of the ranch hands would stop me. They said I wasn't welcome on the ranch, and they'd call the sheriff if I came again. But I did return. I'd leave a letter for you each visit. The letters included my phone number and address. I never heard back."

"I never saw any letters." Virgil lowered himself into a chair.

"I know." She sat down in one of the chairs. "Jasper told me he had no intention of ever showing them to you.

That's when I stopped writing. By then, you were twelve. He did read them for himself, though."

"Did he tell you that?"

"He didn't have to. Jasper used the address in my letters to send me news of you. It's how I knew about you and Lily. What he didn't know was I used to ride to the ranch on horseback. I'd watch you from a post near Whistle Rock. Most times, you were with Wyatt." A small smile tipped up the corners of her mouth. "I was at your high school graduation, and many of the rodeos you competed in. I even drove to Laramie when you left for college."

Burying his face in his hands, he let out an animalistic groan. Lily walked to him, placing a hand on his shoulder. The three shared an uncomfortable silence.

Dropping his hands to his lap, he looked at Monica. "Does he still have the letters?"

"I believe so." Clutching her hands together, she rocked forward. "If I had the money, I would've taken Jasper to court. I did meet with an attorney who suggested I file kidnapping charges against him. She felt confident I'd win. I couldn't do it." A tear she could no longer contain rolled down her cheek. "I've always loved you, Virgil. Not a day went by I didn't think of you."

The door to the office opened, a tired Jasper standing in the opening. "What's going on?"

Monica motioned for him to sit down. "Virgil had questions for me. He knows about my visits to the ranch and the letters."

Continuing to stand, Jasper steadied himself by placing his hands on the back of a chair. "I've done many things that were wrong concerning Monica. I should've let her see you many years ago instead of keeping you two apart. There is so much I regret."

Virgil gripped Lily's hand, his gaze shifting between Monica and Jasper. He had no answers for his father's selfish behavior, which cost Virgil a relationship with his mother. Nor did he understand his mother not attempting to see him at school during his rodeo events. Perhaps she knew how Virgil would respond. Much as he had since she came to Whistle Rock Ranch.

Standing, Virgil didn't release Lily's hand as he spoke to his parents. "There's nothing any of us can do about the past. All we can do is move forward, do our best to heal the pain and forgive each other."

Dropping Lily's hand, he knelt by his mother. Taking her into his arms, he fought the tears burning at the back of his eyes. "I love you, Mother."

Monica didn't try to hide her tears. "I love you, too, Virgil. Always and forever."

He tightened his hold for an instant before standing to face his father. "I'll never understand how you could've kept me from her. I do know you've been a good father and teacher. I hope we can speak of this again someday." Hugging Jasper, Virgil began to feel a slight healing in the area of his heart.

Turning back to Lily, he held out his hand, pleased when she linked her fingers with his. "We have decided to marry at four o'clock in two days at the park in town. We've only invited Wyatt, Daisy, Anson, and Margie. If you're available, Lily and I would welcome your presence."

"Are you ready, Lily? We're going to be late." Daisy waited in her friend's living room. Next to her was a box holding four bouquets. One each for Lily, Daisy, Monica, and Margie.

"I'm ready." She wore the same red sundress, sandals, and swing sweater.

"You look amazing." Holding up the professional camera she rarely left behind, Daisy snapped off several photos. "Let's go. I'll drive."

Lily and Virgil had met at the county clerk's office the day before to obtain their license. Today, they'd meet at the park. Daisy found a parking spot next to Virgil's truck.

"I can't believe this is happening after all these years." Lily breathed in and out, trying to calm her racing heart. "I love him so much, Daisy."

"I know." Leaning over the console, she gave her friend a hug. "Are you ready?"

"Definitely."

Less than twenty minutes later, Virgil slipped a ring on Lily's finger before giving her a long kiss. The women swiped at tears while the men whooped in celebration.

In Lily's mind, theirs was the best wedding ever.

Epilogue

One week later…

"Are you sure the guy's going to show up this time?" Virgil walked beside Wyatt to the main house.

"He called this morning, saying to expect him at two o'clock. I'll meet with him first, then pass him along to you."

"Works for me. You may have to find me in one of the corrals."

"I'll call you. That way you can come up to the house."

"Sure hope you like him, Wyatt. If not, we'll need to use Barrel until we find someone."

"I've got a good feeling about him."

Virgil chuckled. "Yeah. I've heard that before."

Giving a mock salute, he jogged toward the new stables. Inside were the horses they'd identified as being perfect for trail rides. Most could handle beginners through experienced riders. The tack had been sorted, cleaned, and organized, including saddles of various sizes.

With Jonah and Gage home, they'd made final decisions about the schedule. The second three weeks were almost full, and Jonah was close to opening the next three.

Gage spent his days preparing the canoes, tents, camping and hiking gear for use by the customers. Routes had been planned out, along with alternatives.

The ranch hands had been schooled on explaining the various activities of a working ranch, as well as what and what not to say to their guests.

The mood around the ranch had gone from busy to almost frenetic with guests arriving in one week. Nacho and Emma had the kitchen humming as they tested recipes. The large storeroom had been rearranged and filled with supplies. They'd even hired a ranch hand with a background as an EMT.

The news of Virgil and Lily's marriage had surprised few people. They planned to have a reception at the end of the season, when all the guests had returned home.

When his phone rang, Virgil wasn't surprised to see Wyatt's image. "Yeah?"

"This guy is perfect for us. He's got everything we could ever want. Guess I didn't remember he'd spent years rodeoing."

"Personality?"

"Open and friendly. Very outgoing. Gage may even want to use him for some of his activities."

"Single?" Virgil asked.

"Yep. And he can start as soon as we make a decision. Come on up and I'll introduce you."

"Remind me of his name."

"Trace. I can't recall his last name. You on your way?" Wyatt asked.

"I'll be there in five minutes."

Feeling good about the guy he was about to meet, Virgil finished what he was doing, and headed to the house.

Checking the time, he smiled. Lily would be home in an hour. After only a few nights together, he couldn't imagine ever being without her.

Reaching the house, he stomped his boots on the stoop. He'd barely entered the front door when Wyatt walked toward him, the other man following.

"Virgil, this is Trace. Trace. Virgil Redstar, our ranch foreman. Why don't you use my father's office. He and Mom left for town a while ago. Trace, nice to meet you. We'll talk real soon."

"Sounds good, Wyatt."

"Come with me. I doubt this will take long." Closing the door, Virgil motioned toward a chair. "Have a seat."

"I want to thank you for being so patient."

"How's your father?"

"Doing well. He's in a home with people around his age."

"Wyatt said you've done rodeoing. What events?"

"Bareback and saddle bronc."

"How'd you do?"

"Pretty well. Same as always. Win some and lose some."

"Any reason you're not still following the circuit?"

Trace glanced out the window before his gaze settled back on Virgil. "I've been doing it a long time. Even though my head's still in the game, my body is tired. Plus, I'm ready to settle down."

"Wyatt said you have experience with cattle. When was that?"

"My dad ran cattle. Several thousand head. I grew up with them, did every job around the ranch. You won't be disappointed in my skills." Trace offered a slow smile.

Virgil watched him. Some might think Trace cocky. In Virgil's mind, he possessed a good amount of self-confidence. A requirement for anyone who followed the rodeo.

"Did Wyatt tell you about our new venture, and the position we have available?"

"He sure did. I've never worked a dude ranch, but don't see that as a problem. The way Wyatt described it, I'd be working with you to provide trail rides, riding lessons, and the occasional ranch rodeo. I do have experience with all of those."

"There's no glamour here, Trace. The men sleep in the bunkhouse, which has a kitchen. You can prepare your own meals or eat what Nacho, our cook, makes each night. Up to you. We've got a real good crew. Some of the men have been here since Wyatt and I were in high school. It's important we get men who can fit in."

"I won't cause you any problems, Virgil. I'm a hard worker and good learner. You won't be disappointed."

Virgil studied Trace again. He liked him. Still, there was a niggling at the base of his skull telling him he didn't know all he should about the man. Regardless, time was short, if he didn't work out, they could find someone else. Standing, he held out his hand.

"Welcome to Whistle Rock Ranch, Trace."

Rising, he accepted Virgil's hand. "Thanks for the opportunity. I promise you won't regret it."

"Show up tomorrow around seven with your gear. Do you have your own horse?"

"I do."

"We'll find you a stall. I know we have it in the file, but I don't recall your last name."

"Griffin."

A bell went off in Virgil's head. Not enough to worry about.

"Again, we're glad to have you with us, Trace Griffin."

Learn about upcoming books in the **Cowboys of Whistle Rock Ranch series** at:
https://www.amazon.com/gp/product/B09RCQK4TF

Enjoy the Whistle Rock cowboys? Here's another series you might want to read: **The Macklins of Whiskey Bend.**

If you want to keep current on all my preorders, new releases, and other happenings, sign up for my newsletter at: https://www.shirleendavies.com/contact-me.html

A Note from Shirleen

Thank you for taking the time to read **The Cowboy's False Start**!

If you enjoyed it, please consider telling your friends or posting a short review. Word of mouth is an author's best friend and much appreciated.

I care about quality, so if you find something in error, please contact me via email at shirleen@shirleendavies.com

Books by Shirleen Davies

Contemporary Western Romance Series

MacLarens of Fire Mountain

Second Summer, Book One
Hard Landing, Book Two
One More Day, Book Three
All Your Nights, Book Four
Always Love You, Book Five
Hearts Don't Lie, Book Six
No Getting Over You, Book Seven
'Til the Sun Comes Up, Book Eight
Foolish Heart, Book Nine

Macklins of Whiskey Bend

Thorn, Book One
Del, Book Two
Boone, Book Three
Kell, Book Four
Zane, Book Five, Coming Next in the Series!

Cowboys of Whistle Rock Ranch

The Cowboy's Road Home, Book One
The Cowboy's False Start, Book Two

The Cowboy's Second Chance Family, Book Three, Coming Next in the Series!

Historical Western Romance Series
Redemption Mountain

Redemption's Edge, Book One
Wildfire Creek, Book Two
Sunrise Ridge, Book Three
Dixie Moon, Book Four
Survivor Pass, Book Five
Promise Trail, Book Six
Deep River, Book Seven
Courage Canyon, Book Eight
Forsaken Falls, Book Nine
Solitude Gorge, Book Ten
Rogue Rapids, Book Eleven
Angel Peak, Book Twelve
Restless Wind, Book Thirteen
Storm Summit, Book Fourteen
Mystery Mesa, Book Fifteen
Thunder Valley, Book Sixteen
A Very Splendor Christmas, Holiday Novella, Book Seventeen
Paradise Point, Book Eighteen,
Silent Sunset, Book Nineteen
Rocky Basin, Book Twenty

Captive Dawn, Book Twenty-One, Coming Next in the Series!

MacLarens of Fire Mountain

Tougher than the Rest, Book One
Faster than the Rest, Book Two
Harder than the Rest, Book Three
Stronger than the Rest, Book Four
Deadlier than the Rest, Book Five
Wilder than the Rest, Book Six

MacLarens of Boundary Mountain

Colin's Quest, Book One,
Brodie's Gamble, Book Two
Quinn's Honor, Book Three
Sam's Legacy, Book Four
Heather's Choice, Book Five
Nate's Destiny, Book Six
Blaine's Wager, Book Seven
Fletcher's Pride, Book Eight
Bay's Desire, Book Nine
Cam's Hope, Book Ten

Romantic Suspense

Eternal Brethren, Military Romantic Suspense

Steadfast, Book One

Shattered, Book Two
Haunted, Book Three
Untamed, Book Four
Devoted, Book Five
Faithful, Book Six
Exposed, Book Seven
Undaunted, Book Eight
Resolute, Book Nine
Unspoken, Book Ten
Defiant, Book Eleven
Consumed, Book Twelve, Coming Next in the Series!

Peregrine Bay, Romantic Suspense

Reclaiming Love, Book One
Our Kind of Love, Book Two

Find all of my books at:
https://www.shirleendavies.com/books.html

About Shirleen

Shirleen Davies writes romance—historical, contemporary, and romantic suspense. She grew up in Southern California, attended Oregon State University, and has degrees from San Diego State University and the University of Maryland. Her real passion is writing emotionally charged stories of flawed people who find redemption through love and acceptance. She now lives with her husband in a beautiful town in northern Arizona.

I love to hear from my readers!

Send me an email: shirleen@shirleendavies.com
Visit my Website: https://www.shirleendavies.com/
Sign up to be notified of New Releases:
https://www.shirleendavies.com/contact/
Follow me on Amazon:
http://www.amazon.com/author/shirleendavies
Follow me on BookBub:
https://www.bookbub.com/authors/shirleen-davies

Other ways to connect with me:

Facebook Author Page:
http://www.facebook.com/shirleendaviesauthor
Pinterest: http://pinterest.com/shirleendavies
Instagram:
https://www.instagram.com/shirleendavies_author/
TikTok: shirleendavies_author
Twitter: www.twitter.com/shirleendavies

Avalanche Ranch Press, LLC
PO Box 12618
Prescott, AZ 86304

The Cowboy's False Start is a work of fiction. Names, characters, places, and incidents are either products of the author's imagination or used fictitiously. Any resemblance to actual events, locales, or persons, living or dead, is wholly coincidental.